SAMMY

Tim Schaub

Disclaimer

While every attempt has been made to provide information that is both accurate and effective, the author does not assume any responsibility for the accuracy of this information due to the fact that it was provided by a lying salamander and heavily edited by his assistant after I was done writing it.

To Sandra, without whose reluctance to do laundry I never would have met Salmmy.

Whoever coined the phrase 'like herding cats' has clearly never tried working with amphibians wired on caffeine.
-Tim

This book is a complete fabrication written by a mean spirited liar bent on making me look bad. Also, tea is terrible, it's just hot water and leaves. Leaves are for sleeping in, not drinking.
-Salmmy

Salmmy is an untrustworthy little coffee addict who bites.
-Tim

You deserved it.
-Salmmy

Shut up both of you!
-Molly

Contents

Random Unrelated Stories

Full Circle

"Thanks for meeting with me Salmmy I really need your help."
"It's Sammy" he growled, without looking up from his desk
"The L is silent."
Raising his eyes slowly and looking under the wide brim of his
hat he noticed her legs first. It was fairly easy given that she
had eight of them.
"Sammy," she was on the verge of tears and spoke in very
short rapid bursts. "M...my children have been stolen."
Salmmy thought it was an odd choice of words and got
distracted for a moment.
'Stolen, not kidnapped. Or would it be egg-napped...?'
Hoping she hadn't noticed that he had stopped listening,
Salmmy replied absently,
"How many children?"
"A...All of them... they took the whole sac when I was building
us a new web."
Tears welled up in her multiple eyes and she began to speak
again. Whatever she said made absolutely no sense, it was just
a confused mess of tears and babbling. She thrust a small
piece of paper towards him. Not taking the note or giving it so
much as a glance Salmmy replied firmly.
"Look, anyone brave or stupid enough to steal a sac full of a
few thousand hungry baby spiders isn't someone I want to
tangle with."
She rose to her feet, tears streaming down her face, the note
still on his desk.
"B... but the note is addressed to you."
He glanced at the note on his desk then spoke quickly. "Follow
me."
Salmmy led her through his small office and into the shabby
little lobby.
The floor was almost completely covered by a thin grey carpet
and completely covered in dust. Peeling paint with delusions
of being modern art flaked from the wall and fell onto the
cracked, dusty, and uncomfortable couch.
The words 'I QUIT!' were carved on the surface of the desk in

the lobby. Its dark brown surface was covered in other smaller scratches that didn't appear to spell anything.

"Wait here," he said, gesturing towards the paint chip covered couch and grabbing his long duster off the coat rack by the door.

Salmmy was nine inches tall, jet black, and covered in yellow spots. His skin was a slightly duller black than it had been before he moved to Ghara, mostly due to the salty, itchy air. He took an antique flintlock pistol from the holster at his side and checked the powder, before gracefully spinning it around and dropping it effortlessly back into its home.

Salamanders were virtually non-existent in Ghara because of the salt that blew in with the ocean winds. Being at the center of the crescent made it an essential port for trade, being a salty windswept place made Salmmy itchy. The air made him itchy and swimming in the ocean made it worse. Salmmy loudly and repeatedly informed anyone who would listen that the only thing that made his life bearable was coffee.

"I'll deal with you later" he growled in the direction of a large metal cylinder with all sorts of dials and knobs. It sat menacingly on a table against the wall. At its top was a large golden bird of some kind with a bullet hole in it's chest.

"What the hell is that thing?" The spider asked, but Salmmy was already gone.

The note was simple and direct; there would be no ransom, no price. It appeared to be written in haste, but the spelling mistake was intentional, every word was carefully chosen, it had the information he needed and nothing more. Worse still it was in his own handwriting.

> Salmmy, their tail and yours end at the same place. Hurry!

It might seem odd that hurrying for Salmmy involved simply walking instead of trying to start his car. Odd that is until one sees his car. A few sharp metal spikes were all that was left where the canopy had been torn off when he attempted to put the roof down while driving on the highway. Both doors were different colours, neither of which matched the rest of the car. There was also the fact that it hated him and refused to start whenever he intended to go somewhere. Somehow it would start perfectly whenever he was trying to figure out what was wrong with it. Salmmy hated it fiercely and vowed he would never get a used car from a badger again.

On windless days when the sun was high overhead the city of Ghara seemed to shine like a new penny. Today was not one of those days. Salmmy hated his wildly unreliable car a little more as he shielded himself from the skin searing salt with his collar and trudged toward the docks. His thoughts began to wander away from complaining about his car. Ordinarily this meant that he was thinking about coffee - his standard topic of thought. However, recently thinking about coffee had meant plotting his revenge on the coffee machine in the lobby of his office. In this rarest of moments, he was actually thinking about the case.

'How was the note in my handwriting?'
'Who wrote it, and why?'
'Who even knows about my tail?'
'Why would anyone steal a sac full of spider eggs?
Salmmy didn't like coincidences.

> *Actually he doesn't like a lot of things and is a huge pain in the*
> *ass to work with.*
> *-Molly*

The fact that his secretary had quit on the same day that a client had actually come by could, in theory, be dumb luck, but he doubted it. He doubted it for a couple of reasons, first among them being that his office was unmarked and buried behind a network of alleys that were usually full of impromptu and mysterious shops with wheels on them. As a result, his office was impossible to find without a lot of asking around. No one who asked around ever called him Salmmy.

As he got closer to the docks the reeking funk of fish clawed its way into his skull through his snout. He tried breathing through his mouth, but soon discovered that the air tasted like sand, salt, and fish which was somehow worse. The docks were a terrible place.

He knew exactly which warehouse he needed to go to, but he simply didn't want to. Weighing his desire to delay visiting the warehouse against the smell he would have to endure if he kept walking around. He headed straight for the warehouse where he had almost died years ago. It wasn't the first time he had almost died, hell it wasn't even the first time he had actually died, but he still didn't like it.

He had been young and cocky; a long string of luck had convinced him that he was invincible. He'd been working for Felipe 'The Columbian' Mustela for as long as he could remember. At the time that was about a year. It wasn't really Felipe's fault that Salmmy had almost been killed. Accidents happen. From what he'd been told that sort of thing happened to him a lot.

Salmmy could think of much better things to blame Felipe for anyway.

Being completely full of himself he had just walked in the front door of the rat infested warehouse certain that he wouldn't be challenged. He was equally certain that if he was, it would end very badly for whomever tried.

Before his eyes could adjust to the darkness he was cracked across the face with what he later claimed had been a lead pipe.

> *They argued about this for hours, it ended in biting and swearing :(*
> *-Molly*

The 'alleged' lead pipe clattered to the ground. The rat holding it had expected that Salmmy would be knocked backward, or

4

at least fall down, but things, for example salamanders, that can walk up walls tend to be a little hard to knock off their feet. The flash of a pistol in the darkness put an end to any regrets he might have had about his choice of weapons.

The six rats hidden in the darkness rushed forward. They knew that Salmmy's gun only had one bullet and that he had no time to reload. His weird obsession with an archaic and wildly impractical old gun was actually the subject of quite a few debates among the rats.

Debates among rats boil down to biting someone on the rump until they agree with you.
-Molly

Since they had him outnumbered and he was smaller than they were they decided to go with their instincts and rushed madly forward biting anything and everything that got within biting range. The first rat to emerge into the light dropped to the ground with a thud. Blood streamed from the large dent in the side of his head.

Rats are known for being vicious, not for being clever. The sad fact, sad for Salmmy anyway, is that rats are far from stupid. The remaining five paused for a moment to coordinate their attack into a single group lunge. They were a snarling wall of fur, teeth, and claws. Salmmy, holding his pistol as a club, was clearly outmatched.

Rats dropped into disorganized piles before him as he bit, clawed, and smacked his way forward. The other thing Salmmy didn't know about rats, the most important thing really, is that there are always more rats.

It wasn't quick, and it wasn't easy, but eventually the swell of rats brought Salmmy to the ground. Struggling against the impossible mass Salmmy felt claws and teeth tearing away chunks of his flesh. The pain and blood loss were driving him from his body into a pressing darkness. He heard himself screaming with pain and rage. It sounded terribly far away, then it stopped.

Salmmy sat up in disbelief that he was somehow still alive and saw rats chasing his tail across the floor. It danced around and seemed to be provoking them. He was dazed, but he still had enough sense to scramble away as fast as he could.

It had taken a few months. but his tail had grown back. He decided it was better to simply not tell people it had ever happened. Felipe had agreed by saying that no one would believe him anyway, not because tails don't do that but because no one would ever believe that something like that could happen to Sam Black.

It was the first time Salmmy could remember hearing the name. He still wishes he never had.

Fast approaching the warehouse, he noted the thick layer of dust and sand in front of the door; evidently no one had used it in a long time. That meant that whoever was inside had used the grimy tunnels underneath the port. That meant rats. He shuddered involuntarily at the thought, his tail wrapped itself around his leg.

His hands were shaking. He paused for a moment in front of the warehouse, his grip tightened on the handle of his pistol and the shaking stopped. He smiled, adjusted his hat, and walked through the door.

Looking around the long disused warehouse he noticed a few beams of light entering through the worn and broken roof. It was a small bonus that it wasn't entirely dark, he could see in mostly dark fairly well but there had to be at least some light. Noting that anyone standing in the shadows could see him clearly while they themselves remained entirely hidden did not make him feel overly safe, so he decided not to think about it. Puddles of rain shimmered on the floor as he walked confidently forward into the darkness. He certainly hoped he looked confident anyway, since he was actually terrified.

The stale air had no trace of a scent, which was odd as sewer rats tend to carry around a lot more than a trace of a scent. The silence within the empty warehouse was thick and imposing. Salmmy wrestled with the urge to shout 'echo' into the darkness. He was saved from his own lack of restraint by a deep and unfamiliar voice from a darkened corner of the warehouse.

"Oy lizard, glad you finally 'effin showed up. Just fought I should give ya fair warning that I'ze gonna kill ya."
'I hate rats,' Salmmy thought angrily. 'Sounding like a moron isn't intimidating.'
He didn't like having his afternoon wasted. It was one thing to kill him, it was quite another to make him walk clear across town when they could have sent him a note. Hell, they had sent a note. The entire afternoon was wasted.
"You might be surprised to learn that I hear that quite often" Salmmy answered disinterestedly.
There was an unnaturally long pause before the voice replied hesitantly, "I intend for you to suffer first, and for a very, very long time."
'Does he even realize that he just dropped the accent? This guy is the worst actor I have ever heard.'
"I suppose that's good news. Listen, while you seem to have quite a bit of time on your hands, I have a grieving mother in my office who is no doubt ruining my carpet by pacing around with all those damn feet, so if you don't mind I'll be off."
Salmmy turned his back on the rat and walked through the doorway. The sound of hundreds of claws in the darkness made him want to run, or throw up, but to his credit, he walked slowly and calmly until he was outside the door.
Then he ran.

He was forced to stop a few streets later by the fact that he wasn't nearly in the kind of shape he thought he was. Leaning against a wall for a moment, he struggled to avoid throwing up.
An hour later he was walking back to his office and thinking about the case, if he could even call it that. The only really interesting thing was the note. He still couldn't figure out how it was in his handwriting, and why did they want him out of his office all day?
Just outside his building Salmmy stopped and picked up a

feather off the ground.

'That's odd, not many owls in town...'

When Salmmy returned to his office he carefully checked for bugs, but the spider was gone.

Working for idiots

Molly's little office had been a janitor's closet recently enough that it still smelled of chemicals. It was cluttered with various sketches of old things, and the old things themselves. Technically they were relics, antiquities, and artifacts but which deserved which title was a mystery.

"Molly, come here!" The professor's voice echoed down the hall and through her open door. The door still said 'janitor' on the outside, so she never closed it.
Molly looked at the intercom on her desk and frowned. She hadn't actually started plotting to kill her boss, unless you count all the fantasies about choking him to death, there were some schemes but there was nothing as complicated as a plot. Reluctantly she moved the piles of paper off of her lap and stood up, gingerly stepping through the chaos she made her way through the door and into the hall.

The professor wasn't in his office. She was about to look for him when she heard him bellowing from the conference room. "Molly! NOW!"
She hated working for him so much.
In the conference room with the professor was a small and shabby grey hamster.
"Good, finally. Tell Mr. Auratus what you told me about the headdress he sent us."
"Doctor." The hamster corrected.
"Prove it." Professor Dassy snapped back.
Molly sat down and began writing.

"What is she doing?" asked the hamster that claimed to be a doctor.
"She doesn't talk, just read it." Dassy replied.

It's not a headdress, it's a Kokoshnik and It's made with fake pearls.

"So they used fake pearls, what of it?" The hamster asked.

So it is a fake, they didn't have fake pearls 40 years ago...

"I am so very sorry this happened. I'll be happy to return the purchase price."
The smiling hamster looked like a used car salesman.
"Molly, Out. Now!" Professor Dassy growled at her. Molly shut the door behind her and went back to her office.

An hour later the hamster was at her door.
"I'll never be able to sell anything here again thanks to you."

I'm not the one who tried to sell a fake Kokoshnik to the university!

"Neither am I, which is why I am offering you a job. You'll make sure that this never happens to me again. I have a reputation to maintain."

Why me?

"Because I can pay you far less than you are worth and it will still be a raise."
Molly almost explained that she wasn't paid as she was only an intern but wisely decided not to.
"I can pay you fifty a month, plus any moving expenses."

Moving expenses?

"My office is in Ghara."

Three weeks later after an incredibly boring trip across the ocean in the cheapest, most decrepit vessel to ever attempt the crossing, Molly was organizing her new desk.
It was only a few days later that she realized the 'doctor' was a

10

grifter who had only hired her to make sure his frauds weren't discovered.

She had moral objections to selling fakes, but she couldn't afford passage home. Even if she did return to the university professor Dassy was unlikely to give her her unpaid job back. Plus, she really hated that guy.

Reluctantly she had to accept that she was doomed to spend the rest of her life working for idiots.

Over the next few months the types of fakes changed from small value items that sold to museums and universities to larger more artistic pieces that sold for thousands to private collectors.

No matter how much money she made for 'Doctor' Auratus she didn't see a penny of it. She decided it was time to renegotiate her contract.

As soon as she walked into the vault at the back of the building where the doctor spent his days pretending to work he started talking.

"Molly I'm glad you're here. I need your help with something."

Sitting on the desk in front of him was a small exceptionally elaborate urn.

Who are you selling this to? It's a brilliant forgery.

"It's authentic Molly. That's the problem."

How is that a problem?

"The problem is who it actually belongs to. I just agreed to buy it after it was stolen, I had no idea the idiot was planning to steal from Hutch."

Who is Hutch and why is that a problem?

"Right, you're new here. Mr. Hutcheson is a vicious psychopath. He was paralyzed in a gunfight or something a long time ago, and he's old, so he'll probably just send someone to kill us."

Us?

"He wouldn't believe me even if I did tell him you weren't involved."

So what are you going to do?

"Return it and beg for my life. Even if I did run I don't have enough money to run forever."
She stuffed the long letter about her contract back into her pocket. Suddenly she didn't care to renegotiate. Homelessness and poverty be damned, if she survived this she was quitting.

She had a small apartment which consisted of either a bathroom with a bed in it, or a bedroom with a bathroom in it, depending on your point of view. Sleep was proving to be impossible, her thoughts kept coming back to getting killed tomorrow. Also robbing banks... It's weird listen...
'I should go out and do something... I'm probably going to die tomorrow anyway... what can you do without money... I could rob a bank, but I would need a gun... I could buy a gun... but I would need money... damnit, the bank again...'
The doorbell rang and for a second she was happy to have a distraction. Then she was curious about who would be at her door in the middle of the night. She wished she had a gun, and ended up thinking about robbing banks again.
The doorbell rang for the second time.
Cautiously, she opened the door.

Standing in the doorway was a very large and very sharply dressed weasel.
"I'm here representing a party interested in the urn. May I come in?"
Molly hesitated for a moment, trying to decide what to do.
"Feel free to pursue your employer's suicidal plan to plead with Mr. Hutcheson. However, I would strongly suggest that

you let me in. I can make you a much better offer."
Molly opened the door.

The next morning the doctor was on the phone pleading for his life and clutching a fairly poor copy of the urn to his furry chest. As Molly had guessed, he hadn't noticed.

She left the office with the real urn tucked under her jacket and went to the coffee shop across the street. As usual, the doctor wasn't paying any attention to what she did. In Jake's Cafe she sat in a booth at the far corner. The weasel from the previous night arrived a moment later and sat down opposite her. She set the urn on the table and looked at him expectantly.
The weasel slid a briefcase across the floor with his foot.
"You had better get back. He has an errand for you to run."
The weasel stood up and left with the urn.

When she returned to the office the doctor was pacing around the front room.
"I need you to go somewhere for me" he whispered despite there being no one around to overhear him.
Where?
"I need a courier. If someone is getting killed delivering this urn, I'd rather it wasn't me."
'Damnit,' she thought to herself, secretly hoping the courier was as dumb as the doctor.
Molly took the address, wrote a short note, and headed outside.

She felt quite lucky that a taxi was waiting outside the building. It wasn't easy hailing a cab since she had never learned to whistle. She got in and handed him the address.

"We've got a stop to make first Molly." The driver said as the car lurched forward.
She tried to remain calm and wished she was armed.

"I'd keep your hands where I can see them if you want to keep breathing."

She took her hands out of her pockets and wondered how he could possibly know where her hands were while he was driving. For that matter, how did he know her name?

Emily

The sun climbed slowly over the mountains, primarily because mountains are fairly tall and hard to climb.
Train tracks began to shake softly, much lower to the ground. The sun peered over the top of the mountain for a brief moment before deciding it was a good idea to leap suddenly forward. The sun seems to enjoy nothing more than startling the hell out of a shadow that was just sitting around minding its own business.
In this case the shadow belonged to the Wabash Cannonball, the only train that actually came to the Smultronställe monastery. The rumbling tracks grew louder as the Cannonball came over the edge of the mountain and stopped in the shimmering valley.
Peering from the window was an exceedingly disgruntled Emily. This particular Emily was an adolescent salamander, jet black with yellow spots. She thought the view was breathtaking, if asked however she would have insisted that it was "lame" and "boring" purely on principle. She was after all, almost an adult, and in her nearly two years of life she had clearly seen and learned everything worth knowing or seeing.

She almost felt bad about arguing with her parents when they sent her to live here. Almost. In her defence, they hadn't really sold the idea very well. Basically, her father had simply declared that she was going to 'live in a monastery on top of a mountain where she would have no friends.' Then, like most parents, they relied on the 'because I said so' argument instead of actually bothering to explain anything.

The conversation, if you can call it that, went something like this;
"You're moving to a crummy mountaintop monastery where you have no friends."
"Why?"
"Because we said so."

15

"Why did you 'said so?'"
"Because we said so!"
"And nothing about that argument seems flawed to you?"
"GO TO YOUR ROOM!!!"
Well, that's how she remembered it anyway.

For the entire trip she had been plotting her escape. Now the thought of going back to a dusty city full of grey buildings seemed terrible. Traffic noise and the smell of exhaust didn't compare to crisp clean air perfumed with the scent of flowers. That, and even if she somehow did escape she couldn't go home without being grounded. Or worse.

The monks, or more accurately from her perspective a bunch of chameleons, were standing by the station waiting for her to arrive. They were all wearing shiny robes that seemed to be a little bit of every colour at once. The chameleons were changing colour along with the robes. Distracted by the display, Emily forgot, briefly, to be grumpy and disinterested. As she got off the train she remembered that she was supposed to be miserable and surly, so she folded her arms and made angry faces at them.

If the monks had just shut up and walked, the climb up to the monastery would have taken them about ten minutes. Instead they stopped to point out and name every single plant and animal they passed. To make matters worse the monks had all taken vows of silence so they used a complicated form of sign language that required two thumbs per hand.
For years later Emily would still be unable to talk about strawberries without waggling her hands around and looking stupid.

The sun was high in the sky by the time they finally got to the top only to discover that the top was actually just a ridge surrounding a valley down another equally long and tediously winding path. Why they had not just built a small tunnel through the mountain is probably a matter of record somewhere.

"AAAAUUUUNNNNNNGHGGHGGHHH." is the best approximation of the sound she made that I can spell. If you are really curious, find an annoyed teenager; they all make that sound.

Emily grumbled and complained the entire way down, which also took several hours because there were different plants on this side, all of which apparently needed named and explained in baffling sign language. Emily wondered who exactly the explanations were supposed to benefit, as she didn't understand them and was the only person there other than the monks who were doing the explaining.

Bands of gold and silver were wound around the pillars of the monastery. The domed and glittery roof shone as brightly as the sun and was made of thousands of differently coloured shards of glass. The monastery itself was massive, but it was dwarfed by the seemingly endless gardens surrounding it. Among the flowers wild strawberries grew like weeds, the cloying, sugary scent was almost overpowering.

That, combined with hours of walking in the sun had done very little to improve her mood. More than anything, the entire scene made it abundantly clear that poverty wasn't among the vows the monks had taken.

She reluctantly followed them inside. After four hours of trudging up and down a mountain she really wanted a to sit for a while. Unfortunately for her, there seemed to be a distinct lack of chairs.

The floor inside looked like a giant white seamless canvas, painted by a slowly changing pattern as the sun shone through the glittery glass dome overhead. The sickening sense of movement and what she suspected was a potentially lethal case of heatstroke made her want to throw up a little, or possibly a lot; she wasn't sure how much of her breakfast was still available for vomiting and she really didn't want to find out.

She just needed to sit down for a minute. But there were still no chairs.

She closed her eyes until the room stopped spinning so much.
When she opened them one of the monks was mid sentence,
well, mid weird hand waving anyhow.
She nodded, smiled, and hoped he would go away.
Instead, he led her to a smaller domed room, which was
through a hallway behind a white door on a white wall in a
room that was lit by constantly changing colours. She had no
idea how he had found the door. As she followed him, she
wondered if the monks had been insane when they built the
place or if it had made them crazy afterwards. Not that it really
made any difference to her. She shrugged to herself and kept
following him.

The chameleons inside the smaller domed room were quite
old. Well, they looked old.
It was probably the beards.
The fact that chameleons don't grow hair at all made the
beards seem that much crazier. Emily decided that they were
clearly far more insane than she had initially thought.

There were still no chairs.
They sat on mats.
'They spent boatloads of money on a stupid shiny glass roof
but they draw the line at buying chairs? What the hell is wrong
with these people?' She wondered angrily as she slumped to
the floor awkwardly.
The mat she ended up sitting on was uncomfortable, even as
far as lumpy mats go, but at least she was finally sitting.

A door opened at the far end of the room.
It, like all the doors here apparently, was invisible until it
opened and disappeared as soon as it was closed.
Emily could already tell she was going to get horribly lost, and
quite often.
The oldest chameleon yet, or at least the one who was most
dedicated to fake beards came slowly through the doorway
muttering something to himself. It's possible that he was just

waving the hand not holding the cane around for some other reason but since she had no idea what any of the signing meant anyway it was probably a moot point.

He stopped and stared down at her with his creepy, cone-shaped chameleon eyes.
Emily felt a little awkward and a lot annoyed. She couldn't help being the only one around who wasn't a chameleon. For the thousandth time she wondered what reason her parents could have possibly had for sending her to this chairforsaken place.
She was fairly used to being the only spotted salamander around, but usually there were at least a few other species as well. Being surrounded by just chameleons made her feel a whole lot more isolated than she ever had before.

After a few minutes of confusing hand waving they realized that she had no idea what they were saying and someone fetched a notepad.
When she could finally understand what they were telling her things became a lot more confusing.

'Do you know why you are here?' They wrote.
"My parents are jerks?"
'Who are your parents?'
"Edmund and Janet Caudata. I'm pretty sure they wrote all this down on a form or something before they sent me here."

The chameleons exchanged glances and hand waving. The oldest chameleon started writing things down again.
'And what do they do for a living?'
"Dad's a diplomat and mom's a cop. Why?"
The old chameleon hesitated for a long time before handing her the pad.
'They should have told you...' it read. After that there were a lot of hesitations and dots where he had tapped the pen on the page. Near the bottom, it continued.
'Your father isn't a diplomat. He is the crown prince of Viti.'
'That's ridiculous.' She thought.

She had no idea what a diplomat actually did, and her father never actually seemed to do much of anything. She had always wondered why they had such a nice house, but had just assumed (and correctly) that diplomats were grossly overpaid. "What kind of a country would have him for a prince?" She asked.

When the chameleons made no effort to answer her, she decided to play along, so she asked them something else.

"So why am I here?"

'Because you are his heir. They won't risk having you two in the same place now that you're no longer a child.' The old chameleon scrawled in response.

"So how long am I stuck here?"

The chameleon looked upwards for a few moments while he did some math in his head.

'Just over a year, then your niece replaces your father as heir to the throne. It isn't as long as we had Solomon. We have much to teach you and very little time.'

"Who the hell is Solomon!?" yelled Emily. She looked around quickly, expecting someone to start yelling at her to watch her language. But nobody did.

The old Chameleon just seemed sad.

When he handed back the notepad it said

'The first of them to breathe. He was to be king, but he died a long time ago.'

Author's note:

Salmmy and Molly tell me that since salamanders hatch underwater, so nobody really knows who is the first to hatch, they determine age based on the first to crawl out of the water. It is apparently called their breathday.

The old chameleon didn't take the notepad back. He stood up

and wandered off through the same, temporarily visible, door. The rest of them seemed content to ignore her and kept signing amongst themselves.

After a few awkward minutes, Emily looked around and saw a much younger chameleon standing silently behind her. She thought it was pretty creepy of him to loom there waiting behind her like that, but she was tired and didn't feel like explaining it to him. He extended his hand and helped her to her feet.

The younger chameleon showed her to her room; a tiny dome behind the monastery. There were hundreds of domes just like it. None of them had any markings on them but somehow he seemed able to tell them apart.

As a note to the readers, chameleons are much better at seeing colours than spotted salamanders are, for some reason, this fairly obvious fact never occurred to Emily.

She was absolutely exhausted from a long train ride and a longer insane conversation, so she decided to have a nap. Emily figured that they couldn't expect her to do a bunch of 'monk stuff' today anyway. What exactly 'monk stuff' was comprised of she was not yet sure, but anyway, she was too tired to think about it.

The bed inside her room was perfect, a nice warm pile of leaves.

'Chameleons don't sleep in leaves...' The thought occurred to her rather suddenly.

She sat in the chair in her room for a moment wondering about it before a slightly more alarming thought occurred to her. She was sitting on the only chair in the entire monastery and it was in her room.

In fact, everything in her room seemed to be arranged for a salamander. There was a warm rock, leaves, and a chair with a tail hole. She noticed something scratched into the rock. It was

21

upside down unless you were lying down on the flat top. It wasn't carved with tools; it was scratched into the rock with claws. It looked like it had taken a long time. She recognized the script of Viti right away. Her parents had tried for years to teach her to read and write in the language of 'the old country.' It had always seemed stupid and pointless to her, so it took her a lot longer than it should have to realize that it was her family name.

Caudata

The Silent Elle

It had been three weeks since Salmmy had gone to the warehouse. He had begun wondering if whoever had sent the spider with the note was going to get around to killing him anytime soon, he had things to do after all.

'You could at least call and make an appointment so I don't have to sit around all day waiting. I mean sure, you're going to kill me, but there's no need to be rude about it.' He thought angrily.

Desperate for some distraction, and a cup of coffee, Salmmy tried to reason with the big gold coffee machine that seemed bent on tormenting him. Disappointingly, no amount of scolding and name calling seemed to have any effect. If anything it simply inspired the damned thing to redouble its efforts to spite him.

There were a few unexpected changes to the front room; Salmmy reasoned that his former secretary must have been cleaning it when he wasn't looking. Dust that had previously just been gathering had begun to knit itself into a sort of blanket.

He enjoyed mocking the coffee machine as its habitat slowly decayed into ruin around it but he was somewhat concerned that if anyone actually came to his office they might misunderstand. This was not simply a case of poor housekeeping; this was a war of attrition between him and his accursed metal foe. A war that he was fully committed to winning.

"Clearly you appreciate by now that no help is coming. You should really just surrender." Salmmy said as he tented his fingers menacingly in front of the coffee machine. He had hoped that it would have had enough by now, but the machine's resolve was unchanged.

"You'll break before I do!" Salmmy shouted as he slammed the door to his office.

A few hours later Salmmy woke up at his desk quite startled.

He had heard something from the front room. He was certain of it.

He happily opened the door. Either his pen pal had finally come to kill him, or the coffee pot was ready to surrender. Both options would be a welcome distraction. He could not have expected what he found instead.

He had a client.

Her suit jacket and a knee length skirt, both very black complimented her dark brown skin. It gave a distinct impression of money, refinement, and class. The contrast with the state of the front room was startling. She couldn't have looked more out of place without really dedicating herself to the task.

Unhappily he realised that if she wanted coffee he would have to explain about the war he was engaged in. He hoped that she would understand that this was the machine's own fault.

She silently handed him a note.

'Good Lord, not this again.' Salmmy thought as he looked down at the letter in his hand. It was neatly written in a rather delicate and feminine hand.

> *Salmmy,*
> *I have been sent here by the doctor to hire you. Come with me and he can explain everything. It will save me a lot of time and effort writing it all out.*
> *-Molly Torosa*

"Well that seems clear enough, out of curiosity who is this doctor?"

A momentary flash of annoyance crossed her face before she remembered something and handed him a card from her pocket. The card was printed on a marbled stock, thick and solid, with a watermark image of the front of the shop behind the text.

Dr. Samuel Auratus
Proprietor
Auratus Antiquities Clearinghouse

1217 8th St

Salmmy noted to himself that there was no phone number. Momentarily he considered removing his number from his own cards, at least until he hired someone else to answer the phone. It never actually rang, but it was the principle of the thing. He could hardly be called a professional if he was answering his own phone.

"Fair enough. Let's go." He waved his hand toward the door indicating for her to lead. She had a great figure, highlighted nicely by her tight waistline; her skirt was slit just enough draw his attention to a lithe and perfect tail that demanded a moment of his time. He was more than happy to spare it. Almost forgetting to grab his jacket, Salmmy followed her through the doorway. When they had reached the basement garage Molly gestured towards his car.
"No." Was all he said.

As they walked through the maze of alleys between his office and the street they made idle conversation. Well, Salmmy did anyway. Molly seemed determined to ignore him and appear annoyed. When they finally reached the street she extended her hand and silently flagged down a taxi. She handed the driver another copy of the card when he asked where they were going.

Salmmy studied her reflection in the window, noting her soft orange lips. The colour ran down her neck to her moderately low cut white shirt. Her dark eyes with shining yellow highlights peered at him from behind fairly thick framed glasses.
It was clear she was quite young, and based on the moistness of her skin, either new to the city or the owner of a pool.

Distracted by fantasies of going for a swim he barely noticed that the cab had pulled to a stop outside of an unmarked and rather nondescript building. It bore no resemblance to the image on the card that she had given him.

A single door broke the monotony of the stonework, a shining red rectangle among slate gray with a bronze knob in the center. He had always found that style of door ridiculous. It turned a perfectly good doorknob into a completely useless piece of door jewellery.

Molly walked up to the door and opened it, pushing Salmmy inside. He would have preferred to follow her, but that was an argument he didn't want to have. She probably wouldn't respond well to his reasons.
They entered a small office with a very old and worn grey carpet. It gave the distinct impression that it had been here since before the building, perhaps since the dawn of time.
'Well, my office doesn't look so bad now,' Salmmy thought, though he knew it was a lie.

Set into the walls were shelves lined with an assortment of trinkets from around the world, most of them were relatively worthless in their places of origin but seemingly impressive enough to pass as expensive. On a desk to the side of a heavy door was a pile of various books, one of which was lying open to a page with a large picture of a Canopic jar.
Molly opened the heavy door, which was not unlike one might find attached to a bank vault, assuming one was sneaking around in places that bank employees would generally frown upon.
As he passed through the door he noted that the lock was intact and undamaged.
The floor and walls of the vault were solid concrete, seamless and unbroken. Two massive lines of rolling shelves dominated the space, one was rolled entirely to the left, and the other was open along the center of the room, exposing a shelf of various urns and the golden bust of some unusually busty pharaoh.

For a few moments Salmmy stood admiring the collection before a stocky greying hamster in a spotless black three-piece suit approached him and extended his paw. He looked more like a high-end used car salesman than an antiquities dealer. His fur was manicured to perfection and the way he looked over his half moon glasses made it clear that they were worn purely for appearances.

"Dr. Auratus, pleased to meet you. Sammy, I presume." The hamsters voice was well practiced and velvety.

"Either that, or whoever does my stationery has a lot to answer for." Salmmy replied dryly.

The doctor waved his paw toward a scattered pile of papers on the bench behind him. "These are the various sketches I made of the jar."

"You have remarkably feminine handwriting." Salmmy remarked as he read the notes on the sketches. "It's surprisingly similar to the writing on the card your secretary handed me at my office."

"You're remarkably observant," the doctor said with a scowl.

"In my line of work it pays to be. Molly said you would explain why I am here. Well, more accurately, the note she handed me said it. Not very talkative that one," Salmmy said.

"Well you see, we don't exactly...own...the urn. That is to say, it wasn't precisely acquired through...legal channels." The hamster replied vaguely.

"I see. Go on," Salmmy replied, rapidly losing interest.

"Well Sammy, here's where it gets a little complicated."

"I see." Salmmy was starting to get a little annoyed.

"It was formerly owned by someone who wants it back a great deal."

"And you can't exactly sell it to him without admitting how you got it, that about right?" Salmmy asked.

"Well, sort of. You see, he knows that I have it already, and since I'm rather attached to breathing, I have decided to return it at no cost."

"So let me ask this another way Doctor. How much is your life worth to you?"

"I can only offer you five hundred dollars."

"Make it a thousand."

"I don't see that I have much choice." The doctor said with a scowl.

"You realize of course that I am not a courier?" Salmmy asked.

"Well, yes, I am paying for your discretion. Something which I cannot count on from a simple courier," Auratus replied.

"Good. And when exactly is this exchange of the urn supposed to take place?"

"Tomorrow." Auratus replied, with a not unnoticeable amount of fear creeping into his voice. "The urn must be delivered to the Hutcheson estate tomorrow at 11."

"Fine. Give me the urn, and the money. I'll take it over in the morning." Salmmy said.

"Well, I don't exactly have the money on me..."

"Well you had better have it by the time I come back tomorrow or I'll break your legs myself. Clear?" Salmmy wasn't thrilled at the prospect of seeing Hutch again. He was the type best avoided by those with a vested interest in their continued existence.

"Y...Yes. Of course," the hamster stammered.

As Salmmy walked out of the vault and across the lobby to the front door Molly handed him a small folded piece of paper. As soon as he was outside, he unfolded and read it.

'Jake's cafe at the end of the block. Ten minutes. We need to talk.'

As he walked to the cafe, he strongly hoped that their meeting would have nothing to do with the urn, but knew that it would. *'No job is ever that simple,'* he thought with a sigh as he sat down in a booth and waited.

By the time Molly arrived twenty minutes later, Salmmy was staring at the empty coffee mug in front of him and preparing to leave.

She sat down without a word and began writing a fairly long note.

"Before you start trying to explain let me save you some time," Salmmy said as he waved at the waiter to bring them two more cups of coffee.

"The urn he handed me is a fake, he doesn't know it, and if I bring this to Hutch he will make sure you both die very slowly. The only thing I need from you is a name. Who did you sell the original to?"

Molly looked across the table, her expression a mix of

confusion and surprise. She handed him the paper with only two words written on it;

'The Columbian.'

Salmmy laughed for a moment before he spoke. "You seriously have no idea who you are playing with do you?"

She looked at him curiously.

"Alright Moll, I'll talk to Felipe and see what I can do. I suggest you go home and pack a bag. You might need to leave town for a very long time."

'It's Molly,' She signed angrily. Angry sign language is an art form that few can master but she seemed very well practiced.

Salmmy stood up without seeming to notice and walked out as the cups arrived at the table.

Reluctantly Molly paid the bill and followed him out the door, just in time to see him disappear in a taxi.

The rabbit Hutch

Several years ago, Frith 'Hutch' Hutchison had been a minor player working for the Vespucci family, running a small crew of other rabbits. He and his rabbits handled the protection racket, it wasn't the 'pay us or something bad might happen' style of protection. Hutch actually had happy customers and took his job fairly seriously. Anyone who bothered any of his 'clients' found themselves on the business end of a very fast-moving heavy object. As a result, he was an oddity among criminals. Often he was recommended to new businesses by their neighbors.

By contrast, the rats went around breaking and stealing things anywhere they found themselves. Anywhere, that is, that didn't have Hutch's protection. It was a little known secret that both groups worked for the same family. The Vespucci were rats, of a sort, not the large vicious local kind. They were far smaller and far smarter. They were Ghara's first taste of truly organized crime.

Those working for the Vespucci family kept their cards pretty close to their chests; anything that got into the hands of the police would get back to 'the family' within minutes through their connections in the department. This turned what should have been a minor problem into absolute chaos. When the dust settled, the Vespucci were dead, Felipe was in charge, Hutch was in a wheelchair, and Sam Black was a legend.

It started with a purveyor of rare and exotic herbs named Duncan. Duncan, as it turned out, was one of Hutch's clients. He had no idea what he was doing when he decided not to pay Felipe for transporting some illicit cargo. He learned fairly quickly that it was a bad idea. Unfortunately for him, he didn't live long enough to do anything with that knowledge.

Hutch was livid. Had he known it could be solved with a phone call, it probably would have ended then and there. If Felipe had known that he had just ordered one of hutch's clients brutally and publicly murdered, he might have been a bit more discreet. Unfortunately, there were a lot of things neither of them knew.

Assuming that Felipe was just another petty criminal who had thought himself big enough to challenge 'the family,' Hutch decided to make an example out of him. This was the kind of thing that he wanted to do personally.

Hutch stormed into a restaurant where Felipe was having dinner and leveled a gun at him. Before he knew what was happening he was staring into the empty black eyes of Felipe's bodyguard who seemed to appear from nowhere.

"Get outta my way. This doesn't concern you lizard," Hutch said, as he pointed the gun at the salamanders face.

"Not gonna happen. I strongly suggest you walk out of here while you can still walk."

Hutch laughed.

The Salamander glanced back at Felipe.

"Boss?"

"He's all yours," Felipe answered without looking up.

As Hutch squeezed the trigger the salamander's powerful tail wrapped around his wrist and lifted him into the air. The bullet went high and wide and lodged itself in a heavy wooden beam. Before Hutch had a chance to react the salamander's gun pressed into his stomach and fired.

Two weeks later Hutch woke up in a hospital, paralyzed from the waist down.

When the Vespucci family heard that it was Felipe that had put him there, they ordered him killed. Felipe had learned who the rabbit was much sooner, and he hadn't been idle during those weeks.

Carefully and quietly he had bought or replaced a few key security people around the bosses. When word of the order reached him he set Sam Black loose. Within three days the Vespucci rats were extinct. Not just the bosses; the entire species.

Entire families were killed in their homes. Anyone even remotely connected with the family was given a choice; die cleanly, or die running. The bosses weren't given a choice. Their deaths were slow and anything but clean.

Everyone knew what had happened and who was now in charge. No one dared to even look like they objected. Sam Black had gone from being an unknown thug to a legend that haunted the nightmares of monsters.

The legend didn't care that Sam hadn't been alone, it didn't care that he hadn't fired a shot, and it didn't care what the truth was. Legends never let the facts get in the way of a good story.

Pop Goes the Weasel

When Molly left the coffee shop, the same taxi with the rat driver was waiting out front. She certainly didn't want to end up trapped in the car again, so she turned sharply left and walked as quickly as she could without attracting the driver's attention.
She made it ten steps before running into another rat who pressed a gun against her chest.
"Get in the car ma'am. I'm not supposed to shoot you if I can avoid it, but it's up to you."
Molly got in the car.

The taxi drove to a phone booth a few blocks away, which started ringing as they pulled to a stop.
"Answer it," said the rat sitting beside her. He prodded her side with the gun, just in case she considered running for it.

On the phone was the same person the taxi had taken her to see the other day. Not 'see' exactly, she had been blindfolded, but she recognized the voice. It sounded frighteningly like the courier she had just hired.
"Listen very carefully Molly. The man that you have just met with is exceedingly dangerous. So am I. The question you will be asking yourself over the next few months is this; which one of us are you more afraid of? I trust you'll make the right choice. Go home and wait for my call."
The phone went dead.
She tapped the plunger a few times; there was no dial tone.

Felipe 'The Columbian' Mustela didn't have visitors during the day. He generally didn't have visitors at night either, but he was less likely to have someone killed if they showed up at night. That said, the only people who did visit were either stupid, desperate, or both. Them and Salmmy.

Salmmy grabbed his hat and coat off the stand by the door and glanced around the front room. His eyes narrowed as his gaze passed over the coffee machine. In his haste to have a chat with Felipe he had almost forgotten that his hateful shiny foe was still lurking in the lobby of his office. It sat defiantly on the table against the wall, its golden surface buried beneath a layer of dust. The pressure gauge was an unreadable mess and the tiny eagle resting on the top looked sad. That made Salmmy happy.

The prospect of coffee made him delay his journey a few moments. Maybe, just maybe, the machine had relented. Carefully he turned it on and demanded coffee. He didn't actually try to make coffee, but rather chose to shout at the machine and pull a lever at random. This, of course, resulted in nothing but steam spraying from a spout accompanied by a growling noise. Salmmy growled back.

"I'll be back soon, with a crowbar. We'll see how defiant you are then," he said, as he opened the door and walked down several flights of stairs to the garage.

For the next thirty minutes Salmmy attempted to start his car. It started a few times, just to taunt him, before sputtering into silence. Salmmy furiously accused it of being in league with the coffee machine and threatened it with all sorts of terrible forms of destruction.

Cursing loudly, he decided to stop before he lit the accursed thing on fire. He angrily trudged up six flights of stairs to his office intent on taking his frustration out on the coffee machine. Halfway up the stairs he remembered that he had left the crowbar in the car. He shrugged and kept walking.

For a long time Salmmy sat on the couch in his room staring through the bay window. The sky became dark. He hadn't moved since he had sat down - not a twitch, not a tremor. His unfocused gaze absently took in the darkness that replaced the sunset, which had been beautiful. Almost perfect, almost. It never was, and never would be, as perfect as it was during the ritual at Smultronställe.

His cockeyed sarcastic smile never wavered, even as the tears rolled down his cheeks.
Two more hours passed as he stared out the window at the growing number of stars. Without any warning, he just stood and walked down the stairs to the garage. When he turned the key the car sputtered to life with a wheeze and a whine.
After a moment of consideration Salmmy decided that he was a little sad that he wouldn't get to annoy Felipe by showing up in broad daylight. He would have to find some other way to annoy him. His mind swimming with ideas he drove to a small rundown apartment building near the port. It smelled of fish constantly.

'Fish and weasel.'
-Salmmy

Fine, it smelled of fish and weasel. The building was almost entirely vacant. Not many people looking for an apartment have the clanging of boats and the smell of old fish on their list of requirements. It was, however, a perfect place for a smuggler who was once king of the underworld. As Salmmy approached the door a fairly large armadillo nodded at him.
"Back again Sam?"
"It's Sammy." Salmmy growled as he walked past him. He stopped after a few steps.
"What do you mean again?" He asked.
"You were here a few hours ago Sam." The armadillo seemed confused by the question. Salmmy reasoned there was a fair chance the armadillo was just stupid and spent most of his time confused.
"It's Sammy!" Salmmy shouted back as he walked up the stairs.
When he reached the top he could smell blood in the air. He slid his gun quietly out of his jacket, leaned against the wall, and peered around the corner and down the hall to Felipe's apartment.

The door and its shattered hinges were lying on the floor and the wind was blowing through the remains of the doorway, dragging with it sheets of blood spattered paper.
Carefully, Salmmy walked toward the doorway, avoiding the papers as best as he could.

He leaned against the wall beside the door, or where the door should have been anyhow, and slowly extended the tip of his tail across the gap at eye level. If he was going to get shot, he would prefer it to be in the tail, rather than the face. After a few moments of nothing happening, Salmmy entered the apartment. It was chaos. Blood spattered papers blew around in a small tornado of debris.
Salmmy put his gun away. He wouldn't need it. It wasn't loaded anyway. It never was. The main reason he carried it was for its weight. It was reassuring, and also fairly useful when called upon to threaten someone.

Felipe's apartment had a large window; or rather, it had previously had a large window. Now it had a large hole in the wall. The glass on the floor told Salmmy that something very large had come in and taken the window in with it.
Lying under the bookshelf, almost completely hidden by debris and piles of books, was Felipe. He hadn't changed much since Salmmy had first met him. His fur was a lot grayer, though, and he was a lot deader. It was the second thing that bothered Salmmy. He didn't want to leave any evidence that he had been here, but then again he knew how useless the police were. As long as he didn't write his name and address on the wall in blood, he was fairly sure he wouldn't have a problem.

Bracing his tail against the wall, he heaved the bookshelf off of Felipe's body. It turned out to be a bad idea. The few books remaining on the shelf fell as the shelf rose, and the shelf itself split in half down the center. Half of it fell on Felipe as Salmmy stood there stupidly holding the other half. Angrily, he hurled the broken halves out of the hole in the wall, forgetting for a moment where he had parked.

Whoever or whatever had done this had been incredibly strong; Felipe wasn't a small weasel. He had stood nearly ten inches tall and was among the most ferocious creatures Salmmy had ever met. To throw him hard enough to shatter a full bookshelf was nearly inconceivable.

Salmmy rolled him over and checked his pockets for anything that could tell him what had happened here. He found some money and a set of keys. Lying in the blood beneath his body, Salmmy found a familiar feather.

He stood up and looked around again, remembering what he was here for. Pressing firmly on the stones of the fireplace he slid open Felipe's hidden safe. The urn sat inside alone and undisturbed.

'Well I guess knowing you had some benefits after all,' Salmmy thought to himself, as he put the urn in his pocket alongside Felipe's keys.

In the hall outside of Felipe's apartment Salmmy stopped for a moment to think. The city wouldn't miss Felipe. Someone would replace him, and it wasn't that Salmmy would miss him either exactly. Sure, they had been friends, a lifetime ago, but on balance, everyone and everything was better off with Felipe gone. It still seemed a shame not to look into it, at least a little. After all, Salmmy owed Felipe his life. If anyone was going to kill Felipe it should have been him. He walked down the stairs and stopped once more to speak to the armadillo guard.

"When did I come by earlier?" Salmmy asked.

"Just a few minutes ago, before you went up the stairs."

For a moment Salmmy considered the response. While accurate, it was entirely useless. He admired that, in some strange way.

"Ok, let me ask this another way. What time was it when I saw you the first time?"

"A few years ago. You were working for Mr. Mustela before I started. I'm sorry, but I don't remember exactly what time it was. Probably in the evening..."

Salmmy smiled before responding.

"Today, what time was it the first time you saw me today?"

"Oh, that was around noon Mr. B..."

"And what was I wearing?"

"Can't exactly remember."

"Fine, do me a favour and go see Mr. Mustela in a few moments. He has some tidying up for you to do."

"See, this is what you get! I wish the coffee machine could see you now!" Salmmy shrieked in rage at the squashed and dented remains of his car. A large shelf had somehow fallen onto it while he was away. He removed any paperwork containing his name and address from the car. The police were a lot more likely to investigate a dead car than the dead weasel.

Salmmy's new car was parked in the back alley behind the building. Until a few minutes ago it had belonged to Felipe, but Salmmy had the keys, and Felipe wasn't in a position to argue about it.

Salmmy stared at the car for a while, admiring its sharp square lines. Jet black and polished chrome. Best of all, it had no back seat. It seemed like it was made for him, or at least for someone with a sizable tail, unlike the one he got from a stupid used car selling badger he didn't want to name.

When he turned the key, the car started without objection. It had a growl that would make any angry beast proud. When he shifted into gear, it failed to stall or somehow end up in reverse. He decided he was going to like his new car.

Having found the urn as well as a new car, Salmmy was in a pretty good mood all things considered. He planned on celebrating by throwing his coffee machine off the roof. Throwing things from great heights seemed to be working out well today.

As he drove toward his office Salmmy passed the clearinghouse. The lights were on and the door was standing open.

'That's odd, they should have closed hours ago,' he thought to himself as he parked in an alley beside the doctor's car. He got

out of the car and locked the door. He had never locked the doors of his old car. Its lack of a roof made the gesture somewhat meaningless. As he walked toward the shop he noticed a small trail of blood on the wall above the door. Slowly, Salmmy stepped inside.

Molly was standing next to her desk covered in blood. A gun dangled loosely from her left hand. When she saw him she raised the gun. Calmly he looked at her over the shaking barrel and walked forward.

"Relax. Where's the doctor?"

Molly gestured towards the heavy door with the gun. It fell from her shaking hand onto the old grey carpet. Salmmy walked past her into the vault. Inside, he found the doctor in a heap upon the cement floor. Blood was spattered across the room and pooled in a few places on the floor.

Salmmy rolled the doctor over with his tail, careful not to get any of the blood on himself. He turned and walked back into the front room without saying a word or glancing in Molly's direction. He picked up the phone and dialed a number automatically.

"Franklin, has anyone been dispatched to 1217 8th St?"

There was a brief pause as he listened to the response.

"Thanks, I'll be gone before they get here."

He stood in front of Molly and took off his jacket. Looking steadily into her eyes, he carefully wiped the blood off her hands with the inside of the jacket before draping it over her shoulders.

"Molly, you need to come with me."

She looked right through him as if she didn't see him. She just stood staring at the doorway without responding.

Salmmy glanced at the doorway and saw nothing. With a sigh he picked up the rather inert Molly and carried her to the car. Luckily for him, she wasn't very heavy. Heavier than she claimed, but not by enough to be a problem over such a short distance.

He put her in the passenger seat of the car.

"By the way, you're covered in blood, so keep the jacket on until we get back to my office. If you ruin my new seats a murder charge will be the least of your concerns." Salmmy smiled as pleasantly as he could. A momentary pause and a look of curiosity passed over his face before he spoke again. "Stay here for a second, there's something I need to check on." He gently closed the car door and walked back to the building and up the wall. When he reached the roof he saw what he had been looking for. A bloody handprint was drying on the ledge and the trail of blood he had seen earlier led directly to it. Bloody prints led to the center of the roof. Salmmy picked up another, now very familiar, feather and turned to head back to the car. As he neared the ledge he confirmed a very uncomfortable suspicion. The hand and footprints were a perfect match for his own.

Salmmy slowly guided a somewhat calmer Molly to the couch in the lobby of his office. He silently wondered if the bloodstains could possibly make the dusty couch's condition any worse. She lied down on the couch, making no attempt to remove the jacket. Her gun was still in the jacket pocket. 'Damnit, don't arm suspects. We've been over this.' He grumbled to himself. He also wondered why the assistant at an art shop needed a gun in the first place but now didn't seem like a good time to ask. Instead he walked into his office and opened the bottom drawer of his desk. He came back into the lobby with a heavy glass bottle and a pony glass. "Drink this."
Molly sat on the dust-covered couch nursing the drink for a few minutes while Salmmy rummaged around his room. When he walked back into the front room he took her arm and led her through the door into his office. A curtain was pulled back, revealing the shambles that passed for his home.
"The tub is over there; clean clothes are hanging in the closet. I'll sleep at my desk and take you home in the morning." He took his jacket and walked to the front room, closing the curtain behind him. It didn't take long for him to begin dreaming about the place he had called home for so many years.

Dreams of Smultronställe

Salmmy had been living in the Smultronställe monastery for years. Two years, if he thought about it. They used a weird calendar which he never really understood, so he really did have to think about it. By all rights, he should have earned his shiny new robes months ago. The primary reason he hadn't was that not being a chameleon was a pretty big impediment to changing colours.

Most people would have been discouraged by being given an obviously impossible task. They even called him Little Leopard because he couldn't change his spots. Chameleons aren't well known for their wit. It didn't matter to him at all that he would never actually fit in; it was better than the life that he had left behind.

The monks didn't speak at all; they used a complicated sign language that involved changing colours and having an extra thumb. Little Leopard just spoke. It irritated a lot of the stodgier old ones, so he went out of his way to talk to them whenever he could.

Oscar seemed to hate him more than the rest. He wore a very long fake beard and rarely left the inner chamber. This made it all the more surprising for Salmmy to wake up and see him standing over him. He barely had time to wonder what could possibly be important enough that they sent him of all people, when Oscar spoke. Out loud.

"I have a job for you. Follow."

Dozens of questions raced through his head as he hastily threw on his robes and ran after the old chameleon. First among them being; why had Oscar spoken? He wasn't given any response to his questions at the best of times, so he didn't expect much. He still asked as many things as he could think of while Oscar led him into the basement below the monastery.

The colours had been stolen. With only two months before the ceremony, there would be no time to collect more. The monks spent most of the year collecting the various powders and goos which were collectively known as the colours.

They were stored fairly deep underground in big glass cylinders to keep them dry, or wet, as the case may be. Ordinarily the only way into this room was a long stairway accessed from the inner dome of the temple. No one but the elders themselves was allowed into even that room. Today however there seemed to be a new way in. A large tunnel had been dug straight through the mountain and through the wall. Oscar stood silently as Salmmy looked around the room and at the tunnel.

"Find them." Oscar demanded before turning to leave.

"Why me?"

"We both know who and what you are. No matter how he tries a leopard cannot change his spots." He said as he closed the door behind him.

It didn't take a genius to figure out that the tunnel had been dug by moles, they have six fingers that leave fairly distinct marks. At the far end of the tunnel was an improvised train station, the tracks from the monastery only led to one place. The city of Ghara. Salmmy had sworn he would never go back. But it wasn't like he had a choice.

He had to pack quickly, fortunately monks don't tend to own much. Before he headed for the train he took one last look at his room. It had taken some time but it was perfect. The bed of leaves with just the right amount of soggy mud mixed in, the warm rock, the chair he had built. He ran his hand over the name carved into the side of the rock, it had been so very long since it had been his name. He sighed and walked away.

It had been two months since he left the monastery but Salmmy had become quite comfortable saying goodbye to places he had called home.

A Side Note

This section of the manuscript was recorded using voice recognition software, it is included unedited to show the reader what I had to put up with during the making of this book.
-Authors Note

Salmmy awoke to the smell of coffee.
"No I didn't, why isn't there coffee?"
"Because I am busy writing."
"No you're not, you're talking to the computer."
"Same thing."
"Is it, is it really? Also, why isn't there coffee?"
"I just told you, will you please just finish the story."
"I don't know; my memory is a little foggy... Do you think some caffeine would help?"
"If I make coffee will you just sit down and tell me the rest of the damn story."
"I suppose I could, don't forget the cookies though."

I knew the dame was trouble when she walked into my office. Trouble with two capital T's. When she spoke I knew that in this case trouble also had an exclamation point.

"Sammy what are you doing?"
"Nothing."
"Are you adding things to the book again?"
"No."

She had a voice like a gravel truck with a two carton a day habit.
"Sammy the planet has been invaded by aliens and there is no one else awesome enough to save us all, please Sammy we need your...."

"Damnit Sammy, aliens really?"

"I like aliens."

"You watch way too much television; I'm taking away the remote."

"Where's my coffee?"

"It'll be a minute"

"Then why are you back already?"

"I should just stand beside the coffee machine until it's ready should I?"

"She does!"

"Well she's a secretary, that's kind of what they do..."

"Ow Molly stop biting me, Damnit Sammy stop helping! Let go or no coffee."

"That's a lie!"

"Yeah but it got you both to stop biting me. Both of you just calm the hell down and I'll be right back with coffee."

"And cookies. The speculoos ones. Don't try to feed me those arrowroot things again, I'm armed."

"Sammy you are as tall as my foot, that gun is smaller than the tip of my finger, and it's not loaded."

"What's your point?"

"Even if you could shoot me, it wouldn't even be annoying."

"I could bite you."

"And I could just drink this coffee myself and make up the rest of the story."

"You ARE making it up though, have you read this thing. It's almost nothing like what I told you."

"That's because no one wants to read three hundred pages about why the coffee in the shop below your office is terrible."

"You didn't even mention it though, actually I don't think you even mentioned that there was a coffee shop."

"Is it important to the story?"

"I guess not, hey, where's my coffee?"

"Here... can we continue?"

"Fine."

Salmmy awoke to the smell of coffee...

Return the urn

Salmmy awoke to the smell of coffee. Hutch was a dangerous psychopath who would probably have him shot on sight, but Salmmy had coffee so he was happy.

Molly set a cup on his desk and pulled at the shimmering iridescent robe she was wearing while she looked at him curiously.

"Penance Moll, I'd rather not talk about it."

'Molly.' She signed absently as she walked back into the front room and began looking through the drawers at the desk.

Salmmy stood watching her as he sipped his coffee. When she had found a piece of paper she took the pen off the desk and scribbled a quick note.

Why did you help me?

"Molly, you were standing at the scene of a murder covered in blood and holding a gun."

She looked at him puzzled, that was easily the worst answer she had ever heard.

"Do you really think the police would have bothered to notice that the doctor hadn't been shot, or that your hands had no cuts on them?"

Thank you

"Sure. Let's go, and please tell me you packed a bag when I told you too."

She nodded, even more confused.

Salmmy reached for his long grey duster before realizing the inside of it was covered in blood, also Molly's gun was still in the pocket. He'd sort that out later.

Molly directed Salmmy to her house with confusing hand gestures that she assumed meant something to him.

"Do me a favour, just point left or right." Salmmy said

repeatedly throughout the trip.

When they finally arrived there were no police cars in sight.

"Go get whatever you need; I'll wait here in case anyone shows up, try to hurry."

Salmmy found himself sitting in the car for the better part of an hour. Molly, like many women, had the nearly mystical ability to make even the simplest of tasks take forever.

When the door to her small house opened. It took him a moment to look disinterested. The yellow gleam in her eyes shone more brightly than he remembered. Orange lips and a ruby red shawl made her look like living fire. A gold and purple belt wrapped tightly around her thin waist it made the curve of her hips that much more noticeable. He also noticed that her skirt flowed smoothly over her legs, tightening and relaxing with each step. Hoping she hadn't noticed him noticing he spoke with indifference.

"You don't scrub up half bad Moll."

Her expression said that she was hoping for more of a reaction. She however, as usual, said nothing, though she did sign 'Molly.'

"Moll, lean your seat back and stay as low as possible. I have to drop this jar off at Mr. Hutcheson's place and it's best that no one sees you with me."

'Molly!' She signed angrily then began writing on her notepad.

"Spare me the questions and I won't ask where you got that pen."

She stared at her notepad for a minute without writing anything. A few minutes later she picked up the pen again.

"Fine! Hutch knows where I live, if he knows you are with me then he knows where to find you. So just shut up and stay down!" Salmmy growled. Molly leaned back.

Salmmy didn't say another word until they stopped in front of Hutcheson Manor.

"Can you drive?"

She shook her head. It wasn't that she couldn't but rather that she preferred not too.

"They don't have cars in Calay?" He muttered

'What makes you think I'm from Calay?'

"Well, originally anyway... Your accent Moll, dead giveaway."
Molly sat looking confused and annoyed as she watched
Salmmy get out of the car and walk toward the locked front
gate. Standing in front of it were two rather large and not
particularly friendly looking shrews dressed in expensive
looking suits.

"Sammy to see Mr. Hutcheson." He said as politely as he
could.
"The boss ain't feelin well. Piss off." Was the reply.
"I have an appointment."
"I has orders to keep stupid lizards out, so PISS OFF!"
In the years since Hutch had been put in the chair he had been
a persistent thorn in Felipe's side. He had a nearly limitless
number of rabbits and a lot more cunning than anyone had
anticipated. His reach was incredible, Salmmy knew he had to
be very careful.
"Tell Hutch that he sees me now, or he sees Mr. Black tonight."
"I SAID PISS OFF!"
"Tell him." The older shrew barked at his partner.
The younger shrew made a fairly rude gesture at Salmmy and
walked into the house.

When he came back out and unlocked the gate his gaze was
fixed on the ground.
As Salmmy walked past him the shrew muttered something.
Salmmy stopped walking. His eyes narrowed and his hand
pushed his coat away from his pistol.
"What was that?"
"Nothing, he's sorry sir, right this way." The older shrew
quickly interrupted. He led Salmmy inside leaving the younger
shrew to stand by the gate.

Hutcheson manor was absolutely massive; the front foyer
alone was larger than Salmmy's entire office.
The white domed roof was at least two feet high and supported
by gleaming marble pillars that seemed to grow seamlessly

from the marble floor. The windows were covered by white curtains that descended to white couches.

'Trust an animal that can't see colours to decorate and this is what happens.' Salmmy thought to himself.

The shrew led Salmmy to a large set of doors that opened into a solarium full of orchids. He stopped at the doorway and waved Salmmy onward before walking back out to the front gate.

Seated before a large fire was an old greying rabbit in a wheelchair, his paws were tucked into a blanket draped over his lap. As Salmmy sat opposite him he heard a small click.

"Hutch, you're in that chair because you didn't take my advice. I strongly suggest you keep your paws where I can see them."

The rabbit slowly drew his paws from beneath the blanket and rested them on his lap.

"What do you want Black, I heard you retired?"

"Black did retire. Let's start over. I'm Sammy and I brought you a present."

Salmmy set the urn on the rabbit's lap.

"How did you get involved in this?" Hutch asked as he studied the urn.

"I'm not, and neither are you. From the moment I walk out that door this matter is closed." Salmmy stood up and walked toward the door.

He stopped for a moment before opening the door and looked back.

"Out of curiosity, have you talked to Felipe lately?"

"No, why?" Hutch asked suspiciously.

"He's dead. It made me wonder, who has the brass to take a run at Felipe."

"If I knew do you think I would tell you of all people."

"Probably not, that kind of information could be dangerous in the wrong hands."

"Dangerous." Hutch laughed. "With Felipe dead I run this town!"

"Do you? That's good to know. You should talk to Jimmy; he'll be needing a new boss now."

Salmmy walked out the front door and through the main gate

to his car.

As the car drove away the younger shrew looked at the older one and asked.
"Whose mister black? An wide Boss see de liz'rd?" (I should note that shrews are remarkably stupid animals.)
"Not a who. Him a what. Black just a ghost story bosses tell."

When they arrived at the office Molly sat down in the chair in front of Salmmy's desk pulled out her notepad and wrote.

> *What now?*

"Well I am out of a job. It would have been nice to be paid for my time, but that ship has sailed."

> *You're out of a job, what about me? It isn't like I can get a glowing reference from the doctor.*

"That's rough Moll, at least you haven't been charged with anything. Yet..." Salmmy smiled.
Her hand moved almost involuntarily to sign 'Molly' again.
With a sigh she rested it upon her other hand in her lap.
"I'll tell you what, I need a new secretary and you need to stay out of sight for a while. How about we solve both problems and I hire you?"

> *It isn't like I have a choice, should I even ask what the job pays?*

"I wouldn't."

Fire and breakfast cereal

Jimmy had always been one of a kind. A unique and special snowflake according to his mother. He was the type of child who could be innocently making cereal and suddenly the kitchen would go on fire. It didn't help that Jimmy was quite fond of cereal. Among the many reasons Jimmy left home at such a young age was that it was frequently on fire.

Some time in his childhood he had developed a strong dislike for the letter H. Not simply the casual indifference his countrymen displayed by saying things like 'orse, 'ospital. or 'our. Jimmy found that the ' itself left too much of a ghost behind, anyone listening could easily detect the absence of the H and that simply would not do.
So where many folks would say "I'll be there in an 'our" Jimmy would pointedly craft the sentence to avoid his alphabetical nemesis. This resulted in a lot of phrases beginning with 'OY!'. "Oy, I'll be there inna bit won't I." for example.
Friendless, homeless, and suspected of arson Jimmy decided the safest thing to do would be to choose a life that entirely avoided cooking or speaking properly. So he became a pirate.

Sparrows like Jimmy generally try to avoid the open water due to the fact that there aren't many seeds floating around out there, also because they can't swim. After a year aboard the ship he still didn't like looking over the railing. There are very few things in nature as sad as a seasick sparrow.
The ship he served on was named the Corvus. Based in Euston it would sail out to sea and spend a few weeks stealing and reselling all sorts of things. Things people need. Need in the way that rich people seem to be able to need things that no ordinary person has ever heard of and wouldn't want if they had.

On an altogether ordinary day at sea the crew of the Corvus sat lounging on the deck debating whether or not they had scurvy.

Captain Lanny was in the captain's nest high above the deck. Jimmy was fairly sure that it was called a crows nest on ships, but on this one it was renamed by the captain who insisted upon living there. Renaming it made even less sense when one considered that Lanny was a crow.

"Ship ahead, ready cannons!" The Captain's howling shriek pierced every ear onboard. This was fairly easy since many pirates already wore an earring, also because horribly loud and annoying noises come naturally to crows.

The cannons were already loaded. Loaded isn't exactly accurate, packed with seaweed and other things that cannot burn is a better way to explain it.

The reason for this was that when Jimmy had first joined the crew he had been assigned to one of the cannons. After the third or fourth time a rather large fire had mysteriously occurred the crew had decided that the cannons were cursed. Luckily for them no one outside the ship knew the cannons didn't work so they remained quite effective as a threat. No one wanted to try to loot a sinking ship anyway, so it worked out fairly well for everyone.

The captain of the ship they were currently threatening was a tortoise named Yurtle. The jokes about his name ended fairly quickly after he hired his first mate whose name attracted more attention.

Tom, a cat, was both first mate and cook. He had been forced to take the job of cook after he ate the previous one for making fun of his name. Tom didn't do much cooking though, he had an apprentice for that, a small black lizard of some kind that they found hiding on the ship one morning.

After a quick exchange of pleasantries consisting mostly of threats and curses Captain Yurtle surrendered the ship to the pirates without firing a shot. He didn't have any cannons on his ship so really the whole not shooting thing was fairly easily accomplished.

No one on Yurtle's ship, the Freedom, was armed so they

didn't object very loudly when they were rounded up and locked in the mess hall. The grog was locked in with them, the result of which being that both crew and grog were completely drunk in a very short span of time.

Lanny and Jimmy walked around ordering the crew to steal various things before retiring to the captain's chambers in the hopes of finding something decent to drink while their crew finished. Along with a bottle of something very old, very strong, and disturbingly green they found a list of every crewman and what they were paid.
When they had finished drinking the green stuff, and laughing at how little being honest pays, Lanny sent for the captive captain and first mate.

Inside the mess hall the crew were laughing and singing. They knew they would be released eventually, and being only a few days from port they weren't really concerned about starving or anything.
Yurtle and Tom however were not so calm.
"You are sure they won't find it?" Yurtle asked.
"Trust me." Tom spoke confidently as he tapped the small amulet around his neck, with a shake of his head it disappeared into his matted fur.
The door to the mess hall was unbolted and several of the pirates from the Corvus walked in and pointed at Yurtle and Tom. While the door was open a small salamander scuttled out along the roof unnoticed.
Tom and the captain were escorted to the Yurtle's chambers with a bit more prodding than was entirely necessary. It took quite a bit of self control for Tom not to rip the pirates to shreds with his claws.

The tortoise and cat were thrown to the floor in front of Lanny and Jimmy.
"Yurtle, you don't want to die and I don't want to kill you." Lanny spoke softly.
"Good, then don't." Yurtle snapped.

"It isn't really up to me though. I was told to bring Felipe the amulet or your head."

"Those are really terrible options. I don't have the amulet so you will have to bring my head. It will get pretty mouldy by the time you get back to Ghara."

"No need to worry about that, he's waiting for us in Varto."

The pirates tied Tom's paws behind his back and held him down as Lanny picked up a heavy pipe and walked toward Yurtle smiling menacingly.

"I don't have it." Yurtle cried as he was rolled onto his back.

The small lizard was returning from the pirate's ship along one of the ropes when someone spotted the smoke pouring from the portholes and sounded the alarm.

He managed to cling to the side of the Freedom as the pirates swarmed back onto the Corvus to put out the fire.

The door to the Yurtle's chambers flew open.

"Captain, the Corvus is on fire!"

"How? Jimmy is right here!"

"Fire isn't always his fault sir."

"That's what he keeps saying too." Lanny looked suspiciously at the quartermaster and then at Jimmy.

"Take the crew and put it out, then get back here. I want this ship torn apart!"

The quartermaster and the few guards that had been holding the cat ran out the door and down the hall.

"Now where was I?" Lanny kicked some broken pieces of shell aside as he walked toward Tom holding the pipe in his right hand. Tom was watching the pipe too closely and didn't see the large antique pistol in his other hand until it was much too late.

Tom collapsed to the ground and landed on Yurtle. Despite Tom's matted fur being soaked in blood, a small glint of metal caught Lanny's eye as the cat fell.

Captain Lanny ripped the amulet from the unmoving cat's

neck.

"This could have been a lot simpler you know." Lanny said to Yurtle who lay shaking beneath the cooling body of his first mate. Lanny kicked the cat aside and drew a large knife from his belt.

Kneeling over the helpless Captain Yurtle he pressed the knife against his neck so he couldn't retract his head.

"I guess I am bringing him two prizes." Lanny laughed.

The crow looked up when he heard the click of a hammer being drawn back.

The small black salamander standing in the doorway was holding the twin of his now empty pistol, it had been locked in a strongbox in the captain's nest on his ship. Lanny laughed as the salamander fired. The laughter became a gurgling sound as he fell to the ground.

The salamander turned the gun towards Jimmy.

"You're brave, I'll give you that, but you're also stupid. That gun only holds one bullet." Jimmy said to the salamander.

"I only needed one." The salamander answered smugly.

"What's to stop me from killing you then?"

The salamander looked at the dead cat on the ground.

"Honestly I was rather hoping he would." The salamander answered sadly.

Jimmy drew his pistol and fired.

Two days later the Corvus pulled into port at Varto and began unloading cargo. One of the boxes contained the body of a small salamander, an empty pistol, and an amulet.

Felipe 'The Columbian' Mustela had earned his reputation for brutality by handling a lot of business personally. The Vespucci family had put him in charge of straightening out the supply side of their smuggling operations in Varto so he had rented a small apartment that served as a temporary office. When Jimmy walked in with two of the crew carrying a box Felipe looked up with the kind of interest that only comes naturally to apex predators.

"We have the amulet sir." Jimmy said cautiously.

"Where is your captain?"

"I... He... Well you see...." Jimmy stammered uselessly.

The crewmen set down the box and opened the lid.

"Take a few breaths kid, they might be your last." Felipe glared at Jimmy as he spoke.

"He's dead sir."

"How?" Felipe asked.

The response came from the box on the floor.

"He had it coming." The salamander sat up holding the gun and amulet.

"Who the hell is that, and why isn't he dead!?" Felipe roared.

"He was sir, I swear." Jimmy pleaded.

"I got better." The salamander stood up.

Felipe fearsome expression was momentarily replaced with a smile.

"I'm pretty sure this is yours." The salamander said as he tossed the amulet to Felipe.

"Who the hell is he!?" Felipe shouted at Jimmy.

"Some black salamander, according to the list of the crew." Jimmy explained.

"Sam Black, Salamander." The salamander corrected.

"Sam, why shouldn't I kill you right now?" Felipe asked.

"Because I'll get better, and then I'll find you." Sam replied without looking away from Felipe's withering predatory gaze.

"I like this kid." Felipe laughed. "You have a ship to unload captain. Go!" He shouted at Jimmy.

With just a word from Felipe Jimmy became the captain of the largest and most feared pirate crew in the crescent.

A Molly habitat

Molly sat at her desk resigned to the fact that at least for the foreseeable future she would be getting coffee for and putting up with Salmmy. The intercom on her desk made its unpleasant little chirp.
"Hey Moll, can you get me a coffee?" Salmmy's voice asked her through the speaker. Trying not to be disturbed by the fact that he sounded exactly the same as the voice on the payphone she distractedly made a cappuccino.

"Moll, why is there some kind of foam on my coffee?"

'It's a cappuccino'

"So you're saying it ISN'T coffee at all then?"

'No, I am saying it is a coffee with foam'

"Well, coffee doesn't HAVE foam, so I am a little confused as to how this is coffee."

'Just try it'

"And how do you propose I get to the coffee without disturbing the foam?"

'Drink the foam'

"Then why does it have a little picture on it?"

'It's presentation'

"It's certainly presenting a problem, namely that it is between me and my coffee."

'Damnit Salmmy just drink it'

56

Salmmy eyed the cup suspiciously before turning it around and sliding it toward her.
"You first."
She sipped the cappuccino.
"Hmm, so it isn't poison then?"

'Why the hell would it be poison?'

"I don't know, it LOOKS poisonous."

'In your experience how many times has a cup of coffee tried to poison you?'

"Well none yet, but if I were a cup of coffee I could find a few reasons to give it a shot. I mean I am sort of responsible for the deaths of thousands of them after all."

'And if you were a cup of coffee that had decided to poison someone, would you go around wearing an elaborately decorated foam hat?'

"I suppose not..." He stared at the cup for a moment distrustfully then tasted it."
'Well?'
"The coffee is great, I'm just not too keen on my beverages sporting fancy headwear. Can you get me one without a hat?"
Molly stormed away and slammed the door behind her.
Salmmy smiled and happily finished his cappuccino.

Molly was somewhat startled when the front door flew open, not as much by the suddenness of it being opened but by the fact itself. Based on the level of disrepair and dust she had assumed Salmmy never had clients. Her alarm quickly turned to annoyance as the sparrow hopped toward her desk and spoke.
"Ware be that scurrilous scoundrel of a lizard?"
It didn't take a genius to guess who he meant so she simply

nodded in the direction of his door and sat down at her desk to enjoy the garishly behatted cappuccino she had made for herself.

The sparrow pulled a fairly large knife from his coat and waved it in front of her menacingly. She just stared at him and blinked a few times.

"Now don't ye be makin' any noise…"

"She wouldn't dream of it Jimmy" Salmmy said dryly from his doorway.

"So oo's the new chippy?" Jimmy said nodding towards Molly.

"I let you get away with that with the last one because she was a chipmunk and I thought it was kind of funny. Her name is Molly; it would be best for everyone if you remember it." Salmmy responded with a little more hostility than Molly would have expected.

"I'll gut ye where ye stand." Jimmy waved the knife around menacingly then extended his other wing.

"Better birds have tried Jimmy." Salmmy smiled and shook the extended knifeless wing.

"You could've told me Felipe was dead before a damn rabbit just appears on me ship."

"If I had would you or your ship have been there when he arrived?"

"Aye, fair enough…" The sparrow looked downward as he spoke.

While they had been chatting Molly began to hear an oddly rhythmic tapping sound. Salmmy was tapping something on the doorframe.

--- .-.. .-.. -.-- .

Her eyes widened as she realized what he was doing. She looked at Salmmy. He smiled and the tapping changed slightly.

-.-. --- ..-. ..-. . . ..--..

With a glare she stood up and walked toward the bezzera that Salmmy insisted on calling a 'coffee machine.'

"Come have a seat Jimmy, we have a lot to discuss." Salmmy led the sparrow into his office and closed the door behind them.

As soon as the door to his office closed Molly went back to her desk, sat, and finished her cappuccino as slowly as possible before getting up to make the coffee Salmmy had asked for with his tapping.

She opened the door to Salmmy's office just in time to startle Jimmy who was on his way out.
"Have a seat Moll, it's a good thing you made two cups, this might be a touch confusing..." He trailed off as his attention became fixed on the cup she had set on his desk.
"Right, where was I... Well, I was here, but I was thinking about something... Something other than coffee... That's odd, I don't do that often..." His rambling continued for a minute before he remembered what he had been talking about in the first place.
"You have something of a housing problem and I have a rather simple solution."
Molly stared at her coffee and waited expectantly. After a few minutes of silence, she sarcastically wondered if he had any intention of telling her his undoubtedly brilliant plan. She then began wondering if one can actually wonder something sarcastically...
She realized that he had begun speaking again and she hadn't been paying attention. She then wondered if whatever was wrong with Salmmy was infectious or if maybe there was some kind of gas leak in the building. She then realized again that she still wasn't paying attention. She took a long slow sip and looked thoughtful hoping he hadn't noticed.
"So what do you think?" He asked.
'Damn him' she thought, reaching for her notepad.

I don't know what to say...

"Well played." Salmmy smiled.

So where am I supposed to live?

"The flat on the seventh floor." He replied.

What seventh floor?

"The one upstairs obviously."

> *This building only HAS six floors, your office is in the penthouse.*

"We are on the sixth floor, not the top."
Molly took several deep breaths and decided that continuing the 'conversation' was slightly preferable to trying to kill him with a pen. Slightly.

> *So how, exactly, does one get to this mysterious seventh floor?*

"Well, that depends."

> *This isn't funny!*

"It's a matter of perspective." Salmmy smiled and stared into his cup.
"Before you go though..." He glanced at his empty cup and smiled in a way that he certainly must have thought was cute. It wasn't.

> *Go WHERE!*

"To your new apartment... You'll figure it out."

'If it is above this floor, and the stairs end on this floor...' Molly thought for a minute before an idea struck her.
She walked down five flights of stairs and across the large empty lobby on the ground floor. She pushed open the glass doors and looked up at the building.
She kicked off her shoes and began scampering up the wall. As she neared the roof it began to make sense. There were six sets of windows on the building, just the kind of thing one would expect from a building with six floors. The unusual thing about

this building was that it continued onward for quite some time after it had run out of windows. She was fairly sure there was a word for it.

'Forced perspective maybe?' She thought as she reached the lip of the roof.

"So Moll, I noticed you forgot to make more coffee." Salmmy was looking down at her from the rooftop. Molly briefly wondered how he hadn't died from a caffeine overdose before wondering how he had managed to beat her to the roof. She just glared up at him and continued over the edge onto the roof. Other than Salmmy the roof was entirely empty.

She had expected a staircase, or something that would lead into the building. She looked around confused for a moment before Salmmy spoke.

"Follow me."

He lifted a small well concealed ring with his tail, attached to it was a trap door leading to a stairwell.

At the bottom of the stairs Salmmy opened a door into a very well furnished loft, albeit one without windows.

Jimmy and some shrews were busily moving large crates into a pile near a square of floor marked with yellow lines. Jimmy stood next to the pile of boxes and shrews and pushed a button on the wall, the floor dropped out of sight.

"He'll be back as soon as they move those crates, write a list of the things you need from your apartment and I'll have them brought here."

Where does that elevator go?

Salmmy tore the note into small pieces after reading it.

"The garage, and that brings me to your housewarming present. Give me your hand Moll."

She extended her right hand toward him.

"Left Moll, I've seen you write enough notes to guess that much."

She cautiously extended her other hand. Salmmy pulled a small disk from his pocket, it had sort of a bracelet for her

hand that held the metal disk snugly against the palm of her
hand. By pressing her middle fingers against it she could make
a soft clicking noise.

"Alright then, now you won't be a walking paper trail of our
every conversation."

-.-- --- ..- / -.-. --- .. .-. -.. -.. / ..... .- ...- . / .--- ..- ... - / .-.. .. - .-. -
.. -.. / - --- / .... --. -. / -.-- --- ..- / -.- .- -. --- .--

"Is that what you are doing all the time? Flailing your hands
around."

.. - .----. ... / -. --- - / ..-. .-.. .- .. .-.. .. -. --.

She clicked as loudly as possible to emphasize her point in case
the rather rude gesture she made with her finger wasn't
enough.

.-- --- -. .----. - / .. - / -.... / .- / -.... .. - / -.-. --- -. .... .--. .. -.-.
..- --- ..- ... / ..... / .. / .-.. .-.. .. .. -- -.... / - ..... / .-- .- .-.. .-.. / .
...- . .-. -.-- / -. .. --. ..... - ..--..

"Climbing the building and going through the roof would be
rather conspicuous, I'd suggest using the trapdoor above your
desk." Salmmy said as he opened the trapdoor.

.-- .... -.-- / -.... .. -.. / -.-- --- ..- / -- .-- -.- . / -- . / .-- .- .-.. -.- / -
.. --- .-- -. .-.-.- .-.-.- .-.-.-

"Where would the fun be if I had just told you about it?"
She walked down the wall and dropped to the carpet behind
her desk.

Molly stood for a moment looking for something heavy to bash
him with. Not finding anything her hand absently drifted to
her side.

Salmmy was climbing down the wall and facing away from her
when he spoke.

"Your pistol is on my desk, couldn't have you shooting me just
yet."

.-- .... .- - / -.. --- / -.-- --- ..- / -- . .- -. / -.-- . - ..--.. She asked.
Salmmy just smiled at her and glanced at the bezzera and back
at her.

An uncommon owl

Rosco looked down at the roof as he passed overhead. He had been following the pirate bird since the rabbit had visited him on the floating perch.
Standing on the roof was the girl lizard and the 'not father' lizard. Rosco was glad he had seen them using the top door, now he had something to tell father. Watching the 'not father' lizard for the past few months had been very boring. The lizard never seemed to do anything interesting but father made him tell him all the boring things it did anyway.
He was getting hungry now and decided to go home. Father would be pleased with what he had seen today.

Near the edge of the city there was a small hole in the ground, Rosco was sure it had been bigger a few months ago, somehow it seemed to get a bit smaller every day. Had he thought about it he would have noticed that Father did the same thing, but thinking about things wasn't something Rosco generally did.
He landed beside the hole, tucked his wings in and began climbing down.
At the bottom there was a bigger room, it also seemed smaller than it had been. One side of the room was a big window.
Behind the window was father's nest room. Rosco went to the window and tapped on the glass with his beak.
"How big are you going to get?" Father asked as he opened the window.
"Sqwark!?" Rosco answered He was already much bigger than father, and the 'not father' lizard who looked just like him but smelled differently.
"So Rosco what did you see today?" Father asked.

When Rosco was done telling him father seemed tired.
"Sweetie I have a job for you, you like squirrels don't you?"
Rosco nodded enthusiastically.

"Good, I need you to go hunting again. You keep leaving those little feathers everywhere."

Rosco smiled.

Father told him where he could find some tasty squirrels.

Rosco crawled back up the tunnel to the ground and flew into the air.

The end of colour

The chameleons were all busying themselves with pointless tasks. Ordinarily they would be preparing for the sunset ceremony at the end of the month, but the colours had been stolen. Without them there would be no ceremony. Emily had asked about the theft and received the same cryptic response she always received.
"You'll understand in time."
She couldn't use their strange sign language but at least she had learned to understand it well enough to know that the monks didn't make any sense even when you could understand them.
The younger initiate chameleons weren't much better, the only other person who hadn't been through the ceremony before was Kate. At least she seemed sane. Also she would just speak instead of wiggling her weird hands around. One downside was that Kate seemed to have a lot of difficulty not talking.
"So then they smash the snails into a paste and mix it with the red stuff I told you about then they light it on fire then pour it into bowls then they give everyone a bowl then at sunset we all drink it and...."
"Great, but I asked you if you already had lunch."
"Not yet, but thinking about drinking that goo has ruined my appetite, once when I was little I ate a snail, it was gross, have you ever eaten a snail? I prefer flies, they're more of a challenge too..."
"Yeah, that's great Kate, listen I just remembered I have to be at that thing somewhere not here..." Emily walked away as fast as she could without obviously hurrying.

"I know I hired you to be my secretary and everything, but can you do me a favour and stop reorganizing things around here. I like it the way it is." Salmmy whined.

The place is filthy!

"You see dust; I see evidence that I didn't leave my keys there."

So what am I supposed to do? No one ever comes in.

"Oh, right. I actually have a case I was working on before you showed up and distracted me."
Molly wrote angrily, several people had been killed and she was in hiding. Distraction didn't seem to cover it.

Distracted you!?

"Yes." He replied simply.
She forced herself to remain calm.

What was this other case?

"Nothing overly important, saving the world and so on."
Molly gripped her pen menacingly and stared at him, daring him to get off track again.
"There is this monastery up in the mountains a few hours from here. Well, someone stole the colours they need for this ritual. Not so much someone as a group of someones, there are a lot of colours."

Does this have anything to do with those robes you have?

"Same monastery, but no I am almost certain the robes weren't involved. Feel free to question them if you want."
Salmmy was dangerously close to being murdered with a pen but didn't seem to notice.
"They say that without performing the ritual all the colour in the world will fade away."

That's insane, that can't possibly happen.

"Why not?"

We don't have time for me to list all the reasons you can't possibly believe that.

"I never said I did, the point is that they do. Anyhow, the ritual is in thirty days so I should probably stop screwing around and find the colours."

Screwing around? You mean taking cases?

"Call it what you like."

Not the worst dinner

A sharp buzzing sound ripped through Salmmy's office. Salmmy, now covered in very hot coffee, set his cup down calmly. Just as calmly he drew his gun from its holster and bashed the intercom with the heavy handle.
He called out to Molly as he walked to the door separating his office from the front room where her desk sat.
"We need a new intercom, there was something wrong with that one."

Seated on the couch was a smallish blue penguin, taller than Salmmy but small for a penguin. Molly opened the lowest drawer on her desk, full of intercoms, and carried one into his office shaking her head.
"Can I get you a coffee?" Salmmy asked the penguin as he led him into his office.
He just nodded and followed Salmmy into the office where Molly had just finished connecting the new intercom and sweeping the carcass of its predecessor into the bin.
"Be a dear and bring us a few coffees would you."
'Learn to make coffee yourself jackass.' She signed.
Molly just nodded, rolled her eyes, and left through the door. Moments later she brought in the cups, gave a sympathetic smile to the penguin, and gave Salmmy a note telling him where to go and what to do with himself when he got there.
"So, from the beginning..." Salmmy said as he picked up his cup.
He set the cup down quite quickly. The handle was exceptionally hot, almost as if someone had poured boiling water over it. His coffee had a fine layer of grounds floating on its surface.

"My friend Vicente is missing; I just want to know what happened to him. He's a tailor in Pequeño Chile."
"Right, so I assume he is also a penguin? When was the last time you saw him"?

"Yes he is. I saw him about two weeks ago, I dropped off some pants to be altered. A week later I went to his shop and it was closed. I've been back every day since, I'm getting worried."

"About your pants?"

"No! About my friend. Are you making fun of me?"

"Not really, should I be?"

"What the hell is your problem?"

Salmmy looked up from his coffee, past the penguin, and made sure the door to his office was closed.

"No one comes here. I don't advertise. The phone is answered by a girl that doesn't talk. So I really need to ask, how exactly did you end up in my office?"

"El Tero works for Felipe, where else would I go?"

Salmmy worried at his coffee for a moment with a spoon trying to clear a path through the debris so he could drink it.

"So if Vicente is missing, and El Tero is involved, what exactly do you want me to find out? Where his body is buried?" He could have been more tactful but he was still angry about wearing his first cup of coffee instead of drinking it.

"There is a little more to it than that." The penguin continued. "Vicente and his family aren't here legally."

"I gathered that, go on."

"Well Vicente owed a lot of money, smuggling an entire family isn't cheap. El Tero was keeping his daughter as collateral. I think he might have done something stupid and gotten himself killed."

"Happens to the best of us." Salmmy muttered as he spooned more grounds from his coffee. "I still don't see how this involves me in any way."

The penguin hesitated a moment and glanced back to make absolutely sure that the door was closed before he continued "I am supposed to spy on El Tero for The Columbian, there are a few of us watching him as far as I know."

"..." Salmmy waited for him to continue.

"Murdering someone in the middle of the street is exactly the kind of thing I am supposed to report to Felipe."

"Wait, who was murdered?"

"Vicente's partner Jose."
'Who the hell is Jose, not that it really matters.' Salmmy
thought to himself what he said was "Alright, go on."
"And there hasn't been any response to my dead drops."
"Alright, I think I can take care of this for you, go home. Oh
and you were never here, we have never met."
"Molly, let's go out to dinner. Wear something nice." Salmmy
said as he closed the door to his office behind the penguin.

Salmmy sat at his desk absently stirring the grounds around in
the bottom of his cup.
'This wasn't part of the plan, but getting rid of El Tero is
something I'm more than happy to do for free.' Salmmy
thought.
An hour later when Molly returned to the office wearing some
kind of silly tall shoes Salmmy showed amazing restraint by
not being a smartass. He consoled himself with the knowledge
that she now had to wear them down six flights of stairs. They
did have a noticeable effect on the way she carried her tail, an
effect Salmmy noticed several times.

The car slowed down and rolled past a few restaurants before
finally stopping at what promised to be a fairly expensive
place. Molly was beginning to wonder how he kept having
money despite never actually solving, or even getting, a case.
There was a small sign that asked people to wait to be seated.
Salmmy ignored it and chose a table by the door. Molly was
quite surprised when he pulled her chair out for her, in fact
she was growing quite suspicious.

Halfway through finishing eating a wrinkly old penguin
woman waddled into the restaurant. As she passed their table
she slowed and looked at them.
"Tell El Tero that Felipe is dead." Salmmy told her as she
continued walking past them to a different table. She glanced
at the menu for less than a minute before she stood up and
headed for the door. As she passed the bar on her way out she
said something to the bartender to quietly to be overheard.

Molly stopped eating when she noticed him nervously drying the same glass for the fifth time.

"Moll, don't look suspicious, just keep eating." Salmmy mumbled around a mouthful of food.

The barman picked up a phone beneath the bar. It was a very quick conversation, no more than a few words. He hung up the phone and returned to nervously polishing the same dry glass. Less than five minutes later two square shaped penguins walked in and sat at the bar. They spoke for a minute, the bartender handed them a fairly full envelope, and they left. Almost immediately afterwards Salmmy stood up and dropped a few bills on the table.

"Time to go Moll."

She shrugged and followed him, it still wasn't the worst or even the weirdest date she had ever been on.

Salmmy followed a fairly large black car around the area for a few minutes before turning and heading towards the office.

.-- .... -.-- / .-- . .-. . / -.-- --- ..- / ..-. --- .-.. .-.. --- .-- .. -. --. / - .... .- - / -.-. .- .-. ...-.. / .- -. -.. / .-- .... -.-- / .-- . .-. . / -.-- --- ..- / ... - -- / --- -... ...- .. --- ..- ... / .- -... --- ..- - / .. - ..--..

"I wanted them to get a little worried but not enough to stop the car and shoot me." Salmmy replied as if that explained anything.

Salmmy stopped at a payphone. He fumbled with change for a moment before selecting a coin. When he was sure Molly was paying attention he stood outside the booth and pretended to make a call, speaking loudly enough that he was certain she would overhear.

"Jimmy. Tero is taking flight. Should be a sizeable payday." She didn't notice him drop the coin back into his pocket as he got into the car.

The elevator to her apartment was already down when they got out of the car.

"I figured you'd want that; those shoes don't look fun on stairs." Salmmy chirped happily as he bounded up the stairs leaving Molly standing in the garage. She had to agree that coming down the stairs had been really annoying. Then she realized that the elevator was controlled from her apartment, meaning he must have sent it down before they left. Before she had walked down six flights of stairs in the first place. She then realized why he had told her not to bring her gun and why he had just bounded up the stairs so quickly.

'I know where you sleep jackass.' She thought to herself smiling. Her expression saddened as she remembered what she had to do now.

She walked onto the street and handed a note to the driver of the taxi waiting there.

It took Jimmy a moment to respond to the familiar voice on the phone, familiar but somehow wrong.

"Jimmy?"

"Aye?"

"Make sure it's done at sea, no survivors."

The voice on the other end hung up. Jimmy stared at the phone for a moment in confusion

The phone rang again.

He paused a moment as he heard the cheerful greeting, it was the same voice as a moment ago, almost. This time he recognized it immediately.

"Hello Jimmy."

"Sammy?"

"Who else would it be? it's not like you have any friends."

"..." Jimmy waited not wanting to get baited into one of Salmmy's pointless and endless conversations.

"Got any plans tonight Jimmy?"

"Ye just called me an ordered me to do it at sea an leave no survivors. What are ye playin' at lizard?"

"Did I? That's odd. Don't worry about it Jimmy, have a good night."

Flightless birds

Angus was a pudgy, hate filled, evil little sandpiper that had taken advantage of the blue penguins for years. He was in charge of all trafficking for the Vespucci family. Where Felipe smuggled art, he smuggled people. They were a lot alike. The thing that set them apart was that Felipe had Sam Black.
After the Vespucci family had died El Tero, as Angus preferred to be called, made a move to expand into the vacant spaces. Felipe took offence and sent Sam to have a talk with him. Tero arrived in Felipe's office the next day with a broken wing, a large crack in his beak, and an offer. He would stay out of everything but penguin trafficking and Felipe keeps Sam from coming back.
Their deal had died with Felipe. From where Angus stood it was just a matter of time until Sam came for him. So he was cramming objects into a suitcase rather haphazardly while shouting at his son Thomas.
"Because he'll kill us you idiot!"
Thomas wanted to mention that his father constantly claimed to be afraid of no one and to 'run this town' but wisely chose to avoid the inevitable backhand that would cause.
Being away from his father was looking like a very good idea at the moment so Thomas walked up the servant's stairs to his room. He always used those stairs so he could avoid the room at the other end of the hall. He hated that room. It was always full of penguins and the sounds that came through that door had haunted his nightmares as a child.
Now that he was grown he had something new to keep him awake at night. The thing his father was running from. The thing without mercy. The thing called Sam Black.

Salmmy sat watching the sunset through the bay window as Molly was taking forever in the front office. She was supposed to be bringing him coffee. She had a good excuse for taking a while though. For some reason the phone had rung.

When she had gotten over the momentary shock she had picked up the receiver and listened.
When she finally came in with the coffees they were cold. Salmmy read it while drinking his coffee in the most put out manner possible.

Sergeant Franklin called, he said that captain Jimmy's boat had been set ablaze and sank in the harbor. There were no survivors. The few bodies that were recovered had been shot.

The other note she handed him read:

I'm sorry, I know he was a friend of yours

"I knew him, we weren't friends. Best not to read too much into it."
Molly walked away shaking her head as Salmmy muttered angrily about the bezzera being out to get him.

Of Rabbits and Rats

The rats had expanded their territory as quickly as they could, far quicker than they should have. Overnight they had taken over the entire dockyard and most of the surrounding areas. A more prudent animal might have been alarmed at the complete lack of opposition. The rats however didn't see the inevitable coming.

The calls started coming in to the police station just before dawn. Gunfire everywhere. Most of the shots had been fired wildly into the air but the callers had no way of knowing that. No more than the police could have known how many of the calls were placed by the rabbits themselves. In a very short time the rats found themselves engaged in half a dozen standoffs with the police, that's when the fires started.

In one short night of absolute bedlam Hutch and his small army of rabbits had killed ten times their number and secured their place at the top of the criminal food chain. For as long as Hutch was around there would be no challengers. He sat happy and contented in his parlour listening to the radio. The voices of horrified reporters was like music to his ears.

The alarms from the gate and the sound of gunfire ripped his attention away from the radio with just enough time to appreciate the irony that his own compound was almost completely undefended before the large double doors to his parlour flew open.
Staring at the shadowed figure in the doorway Hutch uttered his last words.
"I thought you said you were retired?"
The muzzle flash came less than a second after the response.
"No one retires."

An Idle Molly

The next two weeks passed slowly for Molly. For some reason Salmmy seemed rather insistent that she learn to shoot. She found it especially confusing considering that every time they went out he told her not to bring her gun.

Why don't you want me to bring my gun?

"Because you might shoot someone before I can ask them things."
She couldn't really argue with the logic, but in her defence she hadn't actually shot anyone yet.

The gun in question was a small rather delicate thing with nearly no recoil but he insisted she hold it straight with both hands.
It seemed to her that the only skills she actually needed for her job were making coffee and shooting at tin cans on the roof.
Luckily for her she was rather good at one of those things.
Luckily for the tin cans it was making coffee.
Since the phone almost never rang and the last thing she could even call a case had involved dinner and a really confusing conversation she was becoming quite restless. Deciding to do something about it was easy. Deciding what to do was proving far more difficult.

On one occasion she had tried to get a little creative with the coffee. This had proven to be a rather unpopular decision. She had tried cleaning the office to occupy her time. Unfortunately, this led to another infuriating conversation with Salmmy. It had started when she dusted off the nameplate on her desk and realized it was misspelled.

'Salmmy, the plate on my desk just says 'secratery'.'

"Why is there a plate on your desk? Have you been leaving

dishes laying around?"

'No Salmmy, the nameplate on my desk, it just says 'secratery'.'

"Well what should it say?"

'Molly'

"Good luck teaching it to say that, I am impressed it can say anything actually, not a common skill for pieces of metal to have."
Molly just threw the nameplate in the trash bin next to her desk.

A few hours later she worked up the energy to try and have a productive conversation with Salmmy. It didn't turn out any better than the one about the nameplate.

'Salmmy, I need a new desk.'

"Why?"

'Mine has the words "I QUIT!" carved into it'

"With the exclamation point?"

'Yes, but I don't see how that matters?'

"Well it shows emphasis, although I am not sure how much more emphasis a sentence carved into an oak desk really needs."

'I know what an exclamation point is!'

"Don't make jokes Moll."

She had hoped that having his name written on his door in gold letters might help, it did not. Salmmy noticed that his door now read
Salmmy: The L is silent
"Why is there writing on the door to my office?"

'Because it's your office, your name should be on it.'

"To avoid confusion I suppose?"
'...' She stared at him with now well practiced patience.
"I mean we can't have people accidentally wandering into the wrong office."
'...'
"After all there are countless doors here. Well actually there are only the two, and that one leads outside. Am I wrong in assuming that people would remember having just entered through that door? Or that they would remember that they hadn't just been in my office..."

'Would you like me to have it removed.'

"No, I like it." He smiled and went back into his office.
Molly traced the words carved into her desk feeling more than a little solidarity with their author.

After quite a few of these circular and fruitless attempts at a rational conversation Molly began to realize that one of the only times she ever saw Salmmy smile was when he was being annoying. Salmmy smiled a lot.

The Mole hunt

After a few painfully boring weeks of doing nothing it finally seemed like something interesting might happen.
"I have to go check something out, care to come along?" Salmmy said startling Molly who hadn't heard him come out of his office.
Molly had seriously readjusted her definition of interesting apparently.

As they pulled out of the garage Molly passed Salmmy a note.

'Where are we going?'

"You know I am supposed to be paying attention to the large metal objects around me and not reading notes right?" Salmmy replied before she had even showed it to him.
.-- .... . .-. . / .- .-. . / .-- . / --. --- .. -. --. ..--..
"Thank you, to the Molstat Towers."
.-- .... -.-- ..--.. / .- -. -.. / .-- .... -.-- / .-- / .. / -.-. --- -- .. -. --. /
.- .-.. --- -. -. --. --..-- / .. / -.-. --- ..- .-.. -.. / -.... / .... .. - - .. -. --. / .-
.-. --- ..- -. -.. / -.. .-.. .. -. -.- .. -. --. / -.-. --- ..-. ... . . / .- -. -.. / -.-.
--- -- .--. .-.. .- .. -. .. -. --. .-.-. / -.-- --- ..- / -.-. -. --- .-- --..-- / ..-.
.. .-.. . .-.. .. -. --. / .. -. / ..-. --- .-. / -.-- --- ..- / .-- ....-. . / -.-- --
- ..- .----. .-. . / .- .-- .- -.-- .-.-.-
Salmmy was impressed that she took the time to tap out punctuation.
"The tunnel was dug by moles, six fingered marks on the walls, there wasn't any buttressing so they weren't professional diggers. They stole every single colour, even the worthless ones so they aren't professional thieves either. The lack of mess and the temporary train station means at least someone knew what they were doing. A tunnel that long would have required quite a few paws."
Salmmy turned a corner and headed into the mole ghetto.
.-- .... .- - / - .. .- -. -. -. . . . .-.. --..-- / .-- .... .- - / .- .-. . / -.-- --- ..- / - .-
.-.. -.-. .. -. -. --. / .- -.... --- ..- - ..--..
Ignoring her he continued.

79

"So we are looking for a bunch of moles with free time and no idea what they were stealing. Not because I actually care about them, I want to know who hired them."

... --- / .-- .... -.-- / -- --- .-.. ... - .- - / - --- .-- .-. .... ..-.. / - .... . .-
.. / .- .-. / -- --- .-... . ... / . ...- . .-. -.-- .-- .... . .-. / .. -. / --. .... .-
.-. .- .-.-.-

"Yes, there ARE moles all over the city, and yes in theory they could be anywhere. It just seems a lot more productive to start in the poorest and moleyest part of the city."

.... .- - .---. ... / .--. .-. --- ..-. .. .-.. .. -. --. --..-- / -.-- --- ..- .---. .-
.. / -... .. -. -. --. / .... --. . -.-. ... . -!

"I am not being speciest, I don't even think that's a word!"
Salmmy drove onward ignoring the clicks that became increasingly angry.

They pulled to a stop at the end of a long street, looking out the front window they saw several tall apartment building. Uniform grey, they were only distinct due to the bits falling off of them. Wherever the paint wasn't peeling was probably a window, not that they were easy to spot since they were also covered in grime.
"Notice anything odd about them Moll?" Salmmy asked.

.. --. .... - / .. / .-- .-. .. - . / -. --- .-- / -.-- --- ..- .-. / --- .... / ... --- /
..-. .-. .. --. .-. .- -. / . -..- .-. .-. - . -.. / .-.. --- .-. -.. ... .--.

"YES! You can write now!"
Salmmy looked at her suspiciously as she smiled.
Molly smiled because Salmmy was annoyed, it felt good to be on the other side of that for once.

'It's falling apart and cramped, no one should live there.'

"Well yes, other than that."

'There aren't any lights?'

"Moles don't really use them that often."

'It looks deserted.'

"Considering that about 100 moles live in each building I would call that fairly odd."
Molly stared at him for a moment hoping he would continue explaining and save her the effort of writing.
"Let's go Moll, stay behind me."

Salmmy stood in the courtyard between the buildings for a minute with his eyes closed and his arms outstretched. He turned around slowly for a moment before he opened his eyes and walked into one of the buildings.
The first floor was an empty shell, any wall that wasn't part of the structure had been removed. The floor was covered in scuffs and scratches from long use as a warehouse and garbage was piled in every corner available.

Salmmy went up the stairs first and kept making silly hand gestures back at Molly.
He also seemed to find the most conspicuous way possible to sneak around. He crept along the edges of the hallway to the next stairwell. Molly followed him, walking normally. As they reached the stairs a board beneath her foot squeaked loudly.
"Wait here, I'm going to go play a thrilling round of dodge the bullets, thanks for that." Salmmy hissed bitterly before slowly climbing the stairs, still hugging the wall.

Molly stood at the bottom of the stairs and listened for any sound of movement. She could hear music coming from somewhere upstairs. That certainly explained Salmmy's circling around outside better than her earlier theory that he was just an idiot.

The second floor was much like the first, the doors had been removed from all the apartments and many of the interior walls were removed. The only exception was the door at the end of the hall. The door the music was coming from.
Salmmy stopped beside the door and took a few seconds to calm his nerves before he reached down and turned the knob. The door wasn't locked. The only light came from the windows

above the stairs. It was almost black at this end of the hall. The door opened silently. Salmmy stepped into the doorway and looked around the room, it would have been dimly lit by a single lamp on a table, but fortunately it wasn't on. The phonograph in the corner was softly playing some ancient song or another, it was mostly violins. A mole was sleeping on the couch. A gun lay on the table next to the lamp well out of reach.

"Amateurs," Salmmy said to himself before loudly clearing his throat. The mole shot up and looked at him.

"Sir, I didn't expect…" The mole started.

"Oh shit!" The mole finished as he leapt for the gun on the table.

Salmmy hadn't moved at until he heard the sound of Molly drawing her gun behind him. He threw his arms against the doorframe making sure he was taking up as much space as he possibly could.

A gunshot rang out, the flash left a lingering image of the room. Salmmy's eyes adjusted quickly and he saw the mole lying dead on the floor. He turned slowly and looked down at Molly who was kneeling behind him. The thin trail of smoke from her gun drifted past his face.

"That is exactly why I tell you not to bring your gun with us!" It was too dark to read anything.

..... . / .-- .- ... / --. --- .. -. --. / - --- / ... . --- --- - / -.-- --- ..-

"It wouldn't be the first time I took a bullet, and anyway moles aren't well known for being handy with a pistol, bad eyes and too many fingers."

They looked around the apartment for something that would tell them where the colours had ended up. Moles apparently aren't very bright either, next to the phone was a notepad with an address near the port. Salmmy picked up the phone and dialed from memory.

"Franklin. It's Sammy. I have something for you." Salmmy quickly gave the address and then hung up the phone. After searching the moles body, he walked into the hallway without a word and headed back to the car.

Molly followed after him. He hadn't said anything to her the entire time they were in the moles apartment and kept it up until they were back in their office. Somehow the silent treatment was far more upsetting when the person being silent normally never shuts up.

His former secretary

Something was bothering Molly. It wasn't that she had just killed someone, that would probably start bothering her in a few days. What really concerned her was that she wasn't sure how much the mole had said before she had shut him up. The mole had been in the taxi when she had dropped off her last note. He had specifically asked her to tell him if Salmmy was headed to the towers. There hadn't been time before and he was certainly aware now. Molly had other things to worry about right now; she had a note to write for a cabbie.

Her list of things to do vanished as soon as they came back into the office. There was a young chipmunk sitting at Molly's desk.
"Molly, Pikey. Pikey, Molly. There, consider yourselves introduced. Fill her in on the way." Salmmy closed the door to his office behind him.
"No how are you thanks for doing this. You really are an ass Sammy." Pikey muttered as she stood up and grabbed her jacket off the coat tree.
"We might as well get going, can you drive?" Pikey asked. Molly shook her head.

Idling in the alley behind their office building was a spaceship, well not a spaceship exactly but that was Molly's first impression of Pikey's car.

> *I tend to believe her because unlike Salmmy she isn't glued to my television drinking coffee and rambling about aliens all the time.*   *-Authors note*

The two large doors were about ⅔ of the car. The rest of the car was taken up by the massive growling engine. Shimmering purple, almost black. Soft curves like a flowing liquid. Molly seriously rethought her decision not to drive.

While they drove down the small forest road Pikey held up both sides of the conversation.

"Sorry about the desk."

Molly wanted to stop her and ask why she had quit but there seemed to be no stopping her.

"I was snooping around in my old desk; you have a lot of notepads."

"Did I ever tell you about the time I killed a bear, ok fought a bear. Well, I scared it off anyway, it's a good story…"

Molly had heard the story before, it involved a lot more gazebo accidents and a lot fewer bears than Pikey's version did.

"This forest smells too much like pine, someone should plant cedar or something."

"Does cedar smell like pine?"

After an hour or so Molly suspected that her not talking was one of the reasons she had gotten the job as Salmmy's secretary.

A few minutes later Pikey pulled the car over on the side of the road.

"Any good with a gun?" She asked Molly as she opened the trunk. Inside was a meticulously organized collection of weaponry. Molly stared blankly for a moment as she wondered what exactly the job of secretary covered. Finally, she shrugged.

"Either way take one, hopefully we won't need them. It never hurts to be prepared when dealing with one of Sammy's friends."

Why did you quit?

"Sammy kind of lost it. Felipe told him he was sending some doctor to see him. He said he was going to kill Felipe, there was no way I was getting between those two."

What doctor?

"No idea, a hamster I think."

Molly got back into her seat and stared down the road for a while. Pikey got in and drove, she probably rambled as well but Molly wasn't paying attention.

They had just stopped in an otherwise ordinary bit of forest when a very young and very scruffy squirrel bounded down a tree and onto the hood of the car. He sat staring and waiting for them to get out.

The squirrel had paint stuck in his fur in a bunch of places, it was mostly black and red but there were a few other colours in there for good measure. He wore a bandana that seemed to exist only so he had something to wipe his painty paws on.

"What's with the paint?" Pikey asked.

"Oh, we were making protest signs." The squirrel, whose name was Lars if anyone had cared to ask, answered.

"Protesting what?" Pikey asked.

"Oh lots of things, we have a protest every week before the council meeting." Lars answered happily.

"Does the council ever listen?"

"Of course, who do you think does the protesting." Lars cheerfully replied.

"So you protest an empty council and then those same protesters have a council meeting?"

"Obviously."

"What kind of insane commune are you running here? Who is in charge?"

"We are a Neo-Pagan Anarcho-Collective based loosely on Locke's Treatises, not a commune." He said condescendingly before continuing.

"The council is in charge."

"Uhuh, so who do we talk to about the disappearing squirrels?" Pikey was becoming fairly annoyed with this little squirrel.

"Oh this week it would be me; my theory is that they are being eaten by trees. After centuries of eating their young the trees want revenge. That's why we gave up eating nuts. Everything we eat is cruelty free now!"

Molly stood back a few steps watching the exchange with half hearted interest. If she had learned anything from Salmmy it was that idiots rarely knew what was actually going on and asking them was a waste of time. She walked up a tree and started looking around.

The village, no matter what they called it, was composed primarily of small homes inside trees and long ropey walkways connecting them. The only other structure seemed to be some kind of horizontal flowerpots full of moss.
'So much for cruelty free, being forced to eat that seems pretty cruel to me...' Molly thought to herself.
One of the doors to a little home was standing open. There were painty footprints leading from the doorway to one of the rope bridges. The footprints ended somewhere on the bridge, or at least failed to reappear on the other side.
Pikey and Lars came up a nearby tree and onto the platform Molly was checking for footprints.
"Good, you're here." Pikey said to Molly when she got to the platform. "He says the most recent disappearance was from that house there."
Molly nodded and pointed at the footprints and their absent counterparts on the other side.
"Lars, does anyone ever fall from these bridges?" Pikey asked. Lars just looked appalled.
"Right, squirrels falling from trees isn't very likely..." She was mostly talking to herself.
Molly looked up from the footprints to Lars who was dancing from foot to foot impatiently. She noticed a familiar feather sticking from under his headband.
Taking the feather from him without even acknowledging him she looked at it closely.
"What about it?" Pikey asked.

There are three identical feathers on Salmmy's desk.

"I think we should go." Pikey said looking up at the sky.
"But what about the carnivorous trees." Wailed Lars.
"Stay inside as much as you can and you should be fine." Pikey replied.

"But inside is inside trees. How will that help!"

"Trees are like elephants; they pick things up before eating them. You're safe inside."

"Oh, that's good. Thank you so much!" Lars bounced away happily.

Molly just stared at Pikey.

"Do you really want me to tell them an owl is hunting in their village; they'd probably try to give it a vote or something."

When they got back to the car Molly stood beside the driver's side door and smiled at Pikey.

"I thought you couldn't drive?" Pikey asked as she threw Molly the keys.

Molly caught them, shrugged, and got into the car.

They roared down the dusty road towards the highway. The tires lifted off the ground for a moment as they soared down the onramp. Pikey gasped when she heard the engine revving. The tires bit into the highway and launched them forward even faster. They were crushed against the seats as the car raced onward like a liquid in freefall.

After a terrifying hour the car pulled to an abrupt and somewhat spinning halt in the garage beneath the office. Molly pressed her finger to her lips and tossed the keys back to Pikey. Pikey held her hands together to hide the fact that they were still shaking a bit and did her best to appear as if she wasn't terrified by Molly's driving.

"Tell him it went well, please don't tell him I told you anything else." Pikey said as Molly walked away. She wasn't sure why Molly seemed so angry but she certainly didn't want to be in that office right now. She drove away.

Not our prince

Salmmy was on the phone when Molly stormed in.
"Tyrian purple?" There was a pause.
"Thanks Franklin, remember to keep my name out of it. Load it on the Wabash next week, I'll be there with the snail goo."
Another pause.
"Yes Franklin, they smash snails into a paste to get it, oh is Janet working tonight?"
After a moment Salmmy hung up the phone.
Molly was still standing in the doorway glaring at him.
"Oh calm down they're only snails, and they only feel the first smash." Salmmy said to her.
She threw her notepad on the desk.

What the hell is wrong with you!?

"In general or right now?" He asked, uncertain if she was still angry about the snails.
A flurry of angry hand signs later she calmed down and started writing.

You knew! About the doctor, about Felipe, about the urn, everything!

"So?"

So you didnt do anything to stop it!

"You missed an apostrophe."
She lunged at him with her pen. Salmmy didn't move. She stopped just short of his throat and held the point like a blade against his skin.
"I know a lot of things Moll, that doesn't mean I can do anything about them. For example, I know that you met with Felipe before the doctor died, I know that whoever killed them left you alive, and I know that you have been dropping off

messages with a rat cabbie."

Molly pulled the pen away but didn't put it down.

"So I know you're spying on me for someone dangerous enough to put down Felipe, Jimmy, and Hutch. Should I have done something to stop that too?"

The pen clattered to the floor.

"You know better than anyone that I don't need a secretary, assistant, or whatever else. Other than getting coffee the only job you've had is feeding your mystery cabbie the information I needed him to have."

Salmmy's expression hadn't changed at all, he still had the same idiot grin on his face.

"That said, you are observant and clever, learn to shoot straight and you'll make a decent detective."

'What!?' She signed and looked confused.

"You're going to figure this out in the next few hours anyway so... This office, the agency, me, all of it was set up as a front for Felipe. Your apartment was used as storage for particularly expensive items, Pikey and I were supposed to be keeping each other honest. One day he told me he was sending me a client so he could keep loose ends to a minimum. This client was going to send me to see Hutch. Well I thought Felipe was setting me up to get killed. So I went to see him right after I met with you and the doctor. When I showed up he was dead, so I went back to the doctor, he was dead too, and you were standing there."

With a quick flick of her wrist Molly produced another pen seemingly from nowhere. Holding it to the notepad she couldn't think of anything to say.

"The point is, after tonight there is a very good chance you'll be unemployed. Unless I miss my guess I'm walking into a trap and will end up dead."

So when you're dead I get the office?

"Thanks for the vote of confidence Moll." Salmmy replied with an exaggerated eye roll.

Molly started looking around intently.

"Stop picking new colours, I'm not dead yet!" Salmmy whined.

"Things are going to get a little weird in the next few hours, I need you to just roll with it. I promise that if I am alive I will explain all of this tomorrow. Right now we are going to have a chat with the prince."

What prince?' We don't even have a royal family.

"I didn't say he was OUR prince. Let's go, saving the world and all, mustn't be late."

They pulled to a stop outside an absolutely massive estate, pillars everywhere, pointless marble tiles on the driveway, nowhere money could be wasted wasn't gaudy and extravagant.
The guard at the gate looked suspiciously at Salmmy through the car window.
"ID." He stated flatly.
"Just tell Edmund that Salmmy is here to see him." Salmmy said without turning his head.
The guard picked up a phone in the booth beside the gate.
"Someone here to see you sir, says his name is Salmmy."
After a brief pause he continued.
"A salamander, looks a lot like you actually, bit taller though."
He pushed a button and the gate began to open.
Molly thought that it was weird that Salmmy pronounce the 'L'. She had heard him get upset about that countless times.

'Why did you say your name like that?'

"Same reason it's spelled like that; my kid brother couldn't pronounce my name when I left."

'Since when do you have a brother?'

"Since he was born obviously. I'll explain later." Salmmy said as he got out of the car and walked towards the slowly opening double doors on the front of the house.

The throne room was not exactly what Molly had expected. It's hard to pin down what she expected of a throne room found in a residential section of a democratic city state, but whatever that was it wasn't this.

The floor was covered in moss and leaves, tall strange viney plants covered the walls and ceiling. The air was exceptionally damp and the ceiling dripped scalding water every few seconds.

Sitting in a steaming pool of water was a pudgy jet black salamander with yellow spots.

"How?" He said with surprise. "Sam Black killed you, we had a funeral and everything."

"He just killed me a little, I got better." Salmmy said as he walked toward the pool.

Edmund began to stand up.

"Don't get up, there are ladies present. Well one I guess, but it's non zero so I think it still counts." Salmmy continued.

"So about you not being dead?" Edmund asked.

"Yeah, let's keep that quiet alright, our sister likes her job."

"Fair enough. So why are you here?"

"I'm here to do you a favour."

"Oh well that's good. What favour?" Edmund asked as he casually piled bubbles on his nose.

"Making sure Emily is safe. If tonight ends badly for me, you'll be in a lot of danger."

"She's at the monastery, I sent her there a few months ago."

"Good, neither her or Janet have ever met me so he has no reason to kill them, just you."

"Who?"

"Well, me, sort of."

"So you are back from the dead to warn me that you might be trying to kill me?"

"When you say it out loud like that it just sounds crazy. You'll have to trust me."

"So what do you want me to do?"

"Leave."

Childhood memories

When they left Edmund's estate Salmmy drove slowly and aimlessly for a while without saying anything, he seemed lost in thought and ignored the angry notes and clicking coming from the passenger seat.
He was trying to think about anything other than how his night was going to play out.
What he settled on thinking about was how this whole stupid thing got started.

He'd been very young at the time. It's hard to say how old exactly, mostly because he doesn't remember. Anyway it was a long time age, he'd gotten sick of trains after riding them all over the crescent. if it had been a day earlier or later and who knows where he might have ended up.

He was cold, hungry, and alone. It was time to go home. He and his grand adventure were failures. Then he saw her, illuminated by a flash of lightning in the distance. Tall stacks belched smoke as the slow rumble of the boilers echoed in the wind. Salmmy saw before him freedom incarnate. Every thought of giving up and going home vanished in an instant. Getting onboard became everything.

When the ship finally reached port Salmmy made his move. Years of sneaking onto trains made sneaking onto the ship seem fairly simple. Being able to walk upside down on wet surfaces didn't hurt either. He found a warm corner of the ship and fell asleep. Unfortunately, he hadn't counted on the fact that while trains stop in stations with conveniently located cafes. Boats carry food onboard and don't often stop within a convenient distance to a nice cup of coffee. His situation was still marginally better though, he was still hungry and alone but at least he wasn't as cold.

He really was quite hungry when he woke up, so he set off in search of food. The galley was undefended when Salmmy arrived, a stockpile of salted meats and some bizarre hard biscuits were laid out on a table. He descended upon them like a pack of wild dogs. Well not so much a pack, after all it was just him, and he was far less furry than dogs... Ok so not dogs, more like a single starving Salmmy. Had he been more cautious he might have heard the approaching footsteps.

The door opened loudly behind him. A few moments of awkward silence passed.

"Well come on then, it's up to the captain to decide what to do with you,"

The voice was deep and strong, but didn't seem overly threatening. Salmmy turned around, stolen food hanging from his mouth and looked up, way up.

The cat towering above him was one of the largest animals he had ever seen. The casual extension and relaxing of his claws might not have been meant as a threat, but it certainly worked as one. Salmmy decided that now was not the time to do something stupid, he would have time to do something stupid later.

"Mrff?" Salmmy replied, forgetting for the moment that his mouth was full.

The cat simply flexed its claws again in response and gestured for him to go through the now open door. Salmmy walked dejectedly, leaving a small trail of half chewed food in his wake.

They walked through a few narrow halls with walls made of some hard unnatural metal. Wherever one surface met another there were countless rivets, Salmmy tried to count them anyway.

The cat pushed open a door four times Salmmy's height and shoved him through with a kick. The room was entirely empty and made of metal on all sides. Luckily it did have quite a few rivets so Salmmy was able to distract himself for a while. Eventually boredom made him think of escaping. He realized sadly that he was near the center of the ship and the ship was in the middle of the biggest pond he had ever seen. There was nowhere to go. The upside was that he had time to finish his rivet counting.

Several long hours passed before he heard the door being unlocked from outside. The cat walked in first. He had a strange look of warning on his face.

"Allow me to introduce our most illustrious Captain Romastyx Yurtle."

The captain, it turned out, was a massive tortoise. He had hardened leathery skin and hard piercing eyes. He did speak softly for something so big though; he was easily three times Salmmy's size. For a moment Salmmy relaxed.

"Just call me Captain, I don't want to kill you for mispronouncing my name, I have better reasons to kill you."

"Sir, Captain, I was..." Salmmy started to reply.

"SHUT UP!" The sudden change in tone shocked Salmmy into silence.

"You... are a stowaway. No one will know, or care, if I throw you overboard, or as the cook suggested, let him eat you"

Salmmy didn't much care for either option so he chose to remain silent.

"You have one chance, and only one chance to see tomorrow."

Time stretched out very slowly as Salmmy's panicked mind raced, he stood perfectly still, in stupid stunned silence.

Finally, mercifully, the captain spoke.

"You seem to know your way around the galley."

He turned toward the cat.

"Tom, meet your new assistant, try not to eat this one."

A smile crept over his mouth, well it was probably a smile, Salmmy was still thinking about the possibility of being eaten.

Salmmy walked in front of them through the series of halls to the galley. They walked behind him chatting to each other as if he didn't exist.

"You're a dick Rom, he's just a kid. You didn't need to scare him that much."

"What fun is being captain if I don't get to scare stowaways?"

Salmmy had no trouble figuring out which way to go; he remembered the number of rivets.

'Left twenty-nine, past thirty-five, right twenty-five...' He thought to himself.

He ignored their conversation until it returned to the matter of eating him. He really didn't approve of the topic, especially since they were almost at the kitchen.

"I wasn't going to eat him, I'm pretty sure those things are poisonous."

"When has that ever stopped you before?"

Salmmy spent his days fetching food from the high shelves. His ability to walk along walls and ceilings proved quite handy in the kitchen. He scampered along with a clear disregard for gravity while holding various spices and things for the cat. Claws it turned out are much better at chopping things than holding them.

It was a fairly educational few weeks. Tom, the cat, had a habit of narrating his actions and providing explanations for why he did things. It took Salmmy a few days to realize that this wasn't for his benefit; the cat had simply gone mad.

The nights he spent with the crew taught him a lot of things; he learned the enormous pond they were on was called an ocean. He had no idea what that meant, but it was good to know. He also learned that they were headed for a desert, he had no idea what that meant, but after the relentless taunting he had received over the pond thing he chose not to mention it.

Things had gotten a bit dangerous when the ship was boarded by pirates, other than Salmmy getting a little killed it all worked out.

No one retires

They rolled to a stop outside the decrepit warehouse.
Molly sat watching Salmmy stare out the window for a few
minutes before she went for her pen.
"Weird! Roll with It!" Salmmy snapped.
She stuffed the unread note into her pocket angrily.

Are you ok?

After another few minutes of silence Salmmy reached over to
open his door. Molly handed him a different note.

'So what's the plan here Salmmy?'

"Oh it's very simple, he is going to kill me and take the
envelope from my jacket. You are going to take the box of
purple snail goo back to the temple. The rest of the colours are
already waiting at the train station."

'That's a terrible plan!'

"Probably, but things never go according to plan." Salmmy
smiled and got out of the car.
Molly followed him into the warehouse with her hand
clenched around the handle of her pistol.

An aged rat with grey fur and only one eye was sitting in the
warehouse waiting for them. Wordlessly he stood up and
gestured for them to follow him down a ladder that descended
into complete blackness. Salmmy followed him first, Molly
followed Salmmy. They climbed down for what felt like
forever. Molly was thinking that using a ladder was a very slow
and stupid way to go up or down a wall when one could simply
walk. Sadly, it was too dark for her to express this to anyone so
she kept climbing down.
When they reached the bottom it was just a long hallway with

lights mounted on the wall beside torch holders that showed almost no sign of ever being used. Molly quickly wrote something on her notepad and followed them to the end of the hall which branched out in several directions, up and down being among them. The end result being that the hall didn't so much end as become a giant pit with other tunnels leading into it from everywhere.

Molly tapped Salmmy on the shoulder and handed him a short note.

'I'm sorry'

The gunshots were muffled by Salmmy's stomach being pressed against the barrel. For a few seconds they stood at the edge of the pit. Nothing moved and nothing made a sound.

"I told you my plan wouldn't work." Salmmy smiled at her as he fell backwards and disappeared into the darkness.

Molly walked down one of the corridors and into a lavishly appointed office. The walls were covered in bookshelves that were themselves not covered in books as one might expect but rather with odd trinkets without any discernable pattern. The center of the room was dominated by a large stone desk. As she sat down she found herself wondering how they had gotten it through the doorway.

Looking up she saw that the back wall was an enormous window, behind which of course was dirt as they were fairly far underground.

'They must have brought it in through the window' she thought to herself.

The case full of cash on her lap seemed suddenly very heavy. She hadn't been given much of a choice, it was her or Salmmy, but she still felt guilty. The chair on the other side of the desk turned around slowly.

She was momentarily startled, not by the fact that the salamander sitting in the chair looked just like Salmmy, she had gotten used to that. She was startled by the fact that he had been sitting facing a window full of dirt for five minutes while she looked around his office.

'So what now?'

"Now? I go downstairs and kill him."

'He's still alive?'

"Probably, he's remarkably hard to kill."

'So where is the purple goo?'

"It's downstairs, if he is alive I want him to know that he failed."

'So you're not going to let me take it to the temple when he's dead?'

"Why? You don't believe their ridiculous fantasy about the world losing its colours do you?"

'No, but they do.'

"You've been spending too much time with that idiot." He sneered.

It was strange for Molly, looking at his face. He looked just like Salmmy, but there were a few flaws. He almost never smiled. When he did, it was venomous and showed altogether too many teeth to be considered a smile. There was none of the casual and somehow friendly sarcasm in his voice. He wasn't infuriating either. She wondered why that was on her list of his flaws.

'So I guess I should leave.'

"Not just yet my dear."

Molly began writing. He simply continued talking at her.

'I really should be going.'

"When I had those colours stolen I had no idea all my dreams would come true."

'Seriously you shouldn't tell me all of this.'

"Felipe, Jimmy, and Hutch all dead, my rats control everything, and I control them. And it's all thanks to Sammy."

'What possible good could come from telling me this.'

His gleeful boasting continued on as Molly's notes of protest went unheeded.

'You're going to kill me aren't you?'

Deep under the city Salmmy realized that his hands were cuffed around a pipe behind his back. He took this as good news. Not only was he not in fact dead, as he had planned, but in clear defiance of probability he was also awake. The handcuffs and the whole thing with the pipe was a bit of a dark spot, but overall this was going better than expected.
He looked up at the sound of a door opening. Standing in the doorway was, himself. Well clearly not himself, but he was doing a damn good job of looking like Salmmy.
When he spoke he even sounded like Salmmy, a bit angrier and a lot less charming in Salmmy's opinion, but otherwise the impression was bang on.

"It's good to finally see you again Sammy." He smiled menacingly as he spoke. Reaching down he took Salmmy's gun from it's holster and tested its weight.
"Do I really look like that when I am smiling?" Salmmy asked.
"That's your question, not who am I, not why did Molly shoot you, not how are you alive! Nothing else!?" The other Salmmy

shrieked at him.

"No, I'm ok. No, wait I have one. How did you get an owl?" Salmmy replied innocently.

The other Salmmy smacked him across the face with the butt of Salmmy's gun.

Salmmy spat a little blood.

"You insufferable son of a... How can you be such an idiot?"

The other Salmmy paced the length of the room, the sound of his footfalls were drown out by the rumbling of fishy sewage running beneath them and out to sea.

"I've spent all this time worrying about Sam Black. The legendary monster that ended a dynasty! I've been driving myself crazy wondering how such a thing could even exist! And now I find you are you're a complete moron!"

"Legends do have a habit of not being true." Salmmy remarked quietly with a shrug.

"You're pathetic! I wanted to kill the great Sam Black not some brain damaged private dick!"

"Sorry, but Sam retired." Salmmy said flatly.

"No one retires! You're still playing or you're dead!"

The other Salmmy smacked him again, this time much harder. Then he pointed the gun at Salmmy's face.

Salmmy spat a tooth on the ground and looked up.

The other Salmmy pulled the hammer back as Salmmy smiled at him.

"Look I know you have this grand villain speech prepared and all, but can we just skip to the part where I take that gun from you and beat you until your legs don't work?"

"And how do you propose to do that?"

"Poor planning on your part mostly." Salmmy spoke softly, his gaze briefly flicked to the doorway.

"Poor planning! You're cuffed to a pipe and are about to die! So please, please enlighten me you self righteous little prick, where did I make a mistake?"

"There were only three people still alive that could identify Sam Black. Felipe, Hutch, and Jimmy. Do you think it's a coincidence that you killed all three of them?"

"What the hell are you talking about?"

"You said it yourself, no one really stops playing the game." Salmmy continued.

The other Salmmy's pistol was shaking a little.

"Without Felipe and Jimmy no one is organizing the smugglers and without Hutch no one is keeping the rabbits in their place. Most of your rats were arrested or killed the night you took out Hutch. How long do you think the rats you have left will survive in the vacuum of power you created?"

"There isn't a vacuum, I run this city!"

"Really? Who is your contact in Varto? or Euston? or Viti? How do you plan to deal with Tero if he comes back?"

A trickle of blood ran down Salmmy's cheek as he continued.

"Face it, you're an amateur with delusions of grandeur."

Salmmy was losing a lot of blood, but he seemed to be enjoying this.

"If I were you I would be praying that Sam Black doesn't exist. I can only imagine what he would do if some rank amateur was stupid enough to threaten him."

The pistol trembled harder.

Salmmy dropped his hands to his side as he smoothly stood up to meet the other Salmmy's gaze. The handcuffs fell noisily to the ground.

Staring into his duplicates eyes Salmmy slowly and calmly walked forward until the barrel of the gun was pressed against his neck.

"Let me give you a piece of advice, if you take a shot at the king you'd better not miss."

He was shaking weakly as Salmmy took the gun casually from his hand.

"Oh, one other thing, you forgot about was Molly."

"What about her?" He stammered.

"Turn around."

As he turned there was a loud click.

'Two hands, Moll.' Salmmy signed absently as he holstered his gun.

Molly's other hand reached the handle of her gun as the sound of the hammer falling echoed through the room. She kept pulling the trigger a few dozen times after she had run out of bullets.

Salmmy pushed the body off of the metal grid work floor and into the flowing water of the sewer before he stopped at the door and picked up the large box of purple dye. He turned his head and looked at Molly, she was just staring at the body drifting slowly out of sight.

"You coming?" He asked.

Molly hesitated for a few seconds as she pulled out her notepad. She put it away and signed.

'Why?'

"Why not?"

She stared at him for a moment in confusion.

'Hey since when can you understand sign language?' She signed.

"A few years now, I just thought it was funnier this way." Salmmy leaned back on his tail.

'Sammy, how did you get out of those handcuffs.'

"I wind up in handcuffs a lot actually."

'You aren't a very good detective are you?'

"Detective...? Oh right, no not really. But I do have a pretty good assistant." He smiled hopefully.

'What? Why on earth wouldn't you fire me, I shot you!'

"Moll, you've worked with me for a while now, do you really think that that is the worst thing an assistant has ever done?"

She considered it for a minute, for any other employer the question would be absurd but for Salmmy it really wasn't. Then she realised that he said assistant not secretary.

'Did I get promoted?' She signed.

"Sure why not, and I'll double your salary too."

'But you don't actually pay me!'

"You don't actually work though."

'Fair enough but why did you hire me in the first place if you thought I was spying on you?' She signed.

"It should be fairly obvious Moll." He said.

He placed his hand beneath her chin and lifted her face until she was looking into his eyes. He smiled softly and traced a line slowly up her cheek as he looked gazed back at her.

"You make a great cup of coffee."

She punched him playfully in the chest.

Salmmy staggered a bit before throwing his arm around her shoulder and dropping most of his weight on her.

"Speaking of which, let's go home, I'm dying for a cup, or from being shot, I'll figure that part out later." The box dropped to the ground with a thud and somehow he became even more damn heavy.

She scooped up the box of dye from the ground and helped him up the tunnel to the warehouse.

Colours returned

Outside of the warehouse a police car was waiting for them, the officer inside was a young turtle. Young for a turtle was older than most salamanders ever get. The name printed on his shirt was Franklin Yurtle.

They walked from the big front doors of the warehouse toward the car. Molly was doing most of the walking though, Salmmy seemed to have passed out.

By the time they had reached the street a half dozen more cars had arrived. Uniformed officers of all kinds rushed past them without stopping. The turtle had somehow managed to get under Salmmy's other arm and helped Molly walk him to the car. Together they put him in the back seat.

Molly reached for her notepad and found it missing, she started signing hopefully.

"Sorry kid, no idea what you're saying." The turtle replied.

She looked down sadly and reached for the passenger door. Molly just hoped the turtle would drive faster than he walked.

"No dice doll, you've got a train to catch. I'll take care of him." He pointed to the box under her arm.

"And don't worry about him, I'm almost certain he's faking it. He usually is."

Another officer, a black salamander about Molly's height, waved from beside Salmmy's car.

"He won't mind, trust me." She called cheerfully as Franklin threw her the keys from Salmmy's pocket. The name on her uniform was Janet Caudata.

Molly got in the car and sat staring at the turtle's car as they drove off.

They arrived at the station and found a train car loaded with boxes of colours. Molly put the purple with the rest of them.

'Wait here, I need to change." Janet signed to her.

It was only after she was gone that Molly realized she hadn't spoken. Molly smiled.

A few minutes later Janet emerged wearing the same strange iridescent robe Molly had seen at Salmmy's. She tossed one to Molly.

'If you're going to see the ceremony you need to be dressed appropriately.'

Molly thought that the sheer and exceedingly revealing robes were anything but appropriate but changed anyway.

'You can just talk you know.' Molly signed when they were sitting in the empty train car.

'We're not allowed to talk at the temple, might as well start now.' Janet signed back.

'What about Sammy...' Molly started.

'Who..? Oh him, don't worry about him he'll be fine. We're exceptionally hard to kill' Janet answered.

'We?'

'The salamanders of Viti.' She gestured at the yellow spots on her tail and arms.

'I've only ever seen two of them, other than you.'

'Oh who else? I actually thought my husband and I were the only ones in Ghara.'

Molly suddenly realized that Salmmy had specifically made sure Janet wasn't around when they had visited Edmund.

'I don't know his name actually; I was told he was a prince or something.'

'That would be my husband Edmund, we moved here just after our wedding.'

'If he's a prince why do you work? And for the police, isn't that dangerous?'

'I get bored, and like I said we are very hard to kill.'

'That might explain Sammy. He's easily the most irritating person to ever live, I wondered why no one had killed him.'

'Oh?'

'It's like he wants to die.' It had been a while since she had been able to vent so she went a little overboard.

'We'll be in the middle of almost getting killed and he starts being a smartass. The other day I spent four hours decoding this complicated tap code thing just to find out it says "Please bring coffee, Salmmy." He's supposed to be finding the purple for the ceremony to prevent a chromatic apocalypse and he's wasting his time annoying me!'

'That's sweet.' Janet signed back.

'Sweet? It's a justification for homicide!'

'Think about it, the world is coming to an end and you're what he's thinking about, well, ways to annoy you anyway.'

'That's not sweet, it's psychotic.'

'It's a finer line than you think dear.'

Molly decided to change the subject.

'So why are you heading to the monastery?'

'I'm going to pick up my daughter after the ceremony.'

Molly knew that she meant Emily, she also knew that she wasn't supposed to know that, quickly she changed the subject again.

'Anything I should know before the ceremony?'

'Don't look the chameleons in the eyes.'

'Why not?'

'You'll hurt yourself, they have weird eyes that go in two different directions.' Janet signed.

Molly laughed silently.

The train was unloaded by the smallest chameleons Molly had ever seen. They were barely bigger than the boxes they carried. A rope went around their heads to the bottom of the box and another went around their waist and the box. They dropped to all fours and virtually ran up the vertical path to the temple. Molly and Janet followed along much more slowly despite carrying nothing.

When they had finally gone up and down the hill that mysteriously did not have a tunnel through it they walked out into the center of the field before the temple and sat amongst several dozen monks, seemingly arranged at random. It had taken them a lot less time than it had for Emily though because the little chameleons carrying things didn't feel the need to name every plant.

As soon as the boxes arrived at the temple a flurry of activity began. Powders were mixed, things were boiled, other things were ground together on various large flat stones. But eventually, and before sunset the monks brought out small bowls full of a thick pasty substance. It was hot though, so drinking it quickly would burn a tongue, drinking it slowly would force one to taste it. Molly eyed the bowl suspiciously as it bubbled at her.

Glasses of tea were passed out.

At least I'll be able to rinse the taste out of my mouth. Molly thought as she looked down at the entirely unappetizing mess in the bowl.

'Eat that and you will never see a sunset the same way again.' Janet warned.

'Everyone at the temple eventually goes through the ceremony right?' Molly asked uncertainly.

'Yes, once a year to this to replenish the colours lost at night.' Molly thought about Salmmy sitting in his room watching the sunset. She thought about how sad he always looked. She remembered him saying that one day, if he was cruel enough, she would understand why. She tipped the bowl back and drank it as fast as she could. It burned a little and tasted worse than she had expected. She was only able to keep it down through force of will and with the assistance of remarkably strong tea.

More bowls of food, this time thankfully actual food, (primarily worms and crickets) were passed around the circle by the same tiny chameleons she had seen earlier. Molly was amazed by the depths of flavour. The shining colourful spices were clearly magic. Looking up she saw the light slowly withdraw behind the mountaintops. Molly watched in awe as it poured out of the clearing and up the mountainside in clear defiance of gravity. She wasn't sure if gravity affected light but it didn't seem important enough to dwell on.

The absence of light and colour was deafening. Flowers closed and bees seemed to disappear as if by magic. The fading scent of flowers was intoxicating, it slowly slipped away with every breath. Molly breathed in as deeply as she could and filled her lungs with the sweet and beautiful air. It wasn't enough, she kept trying to breath in harder, jealously clinging to the lungful she already had. She became fairly light headed before realizing that she needed to exhale. The world began to spin and a sudden falling sensation made her gasp as Janet caught her in her outstretched arm and propped her back up.

Molly's unfocused gaze fluttered across the suddenly dark and grey landscape. A cold wind howled through her. Behind her she felt the sun rise. Not the sun she had always known but another that lit the world in a spectrum of colours she had never seen before. On any other night she probably would have recognized the moon.

Everything had a halo of a colour that was somehow both orange and purple at the same time. The grass beneath her feet gave off a soft green light that tasted like lime and smelled like thunder. The intense significance of everything was overwhelming.

She tried to stand up and would have fallen forward if Janet hadn't taken her arm and helped her up.

'Good, you're alive. Let's take a walk.' Janet signed.

It took Molly a few seconds to sort out what she had said though as her hands kept leaving streaks in the world as they moved.

'Sounds good.' Molly replied. She stood staring at her own hands moving for a few seconds after she had finished. Janet took her hand and lead her along a path through the hills toward the trees.

The trees hummed softly as they walked past them. Molly stopped to watch them but as soon as she stopped the trees mysteriously stopped moving as well. She experimented with this for a few minutes while Janet knelt beside the path looking at flowers. The path through the underbrush had a slight reddish glow that separated it from the soft green glow of the grass.

Molly followed the path further, Janet didn't seem to notice. Less than a minute down the path Molly came to a pond lying on its side. A dark swirling mirror. She saw herself in the hallway of the Molstat towers. As she watched the image of her dropped to a crouch and fired through the doorway. She saw the mole lying on the floor dead through the doorway as she calmly put her gun away. As she stared she began to see her and Salmmy standing in the tunnel. She saw herself hand him the note, saw herself pull the trigger twice, saw him fall. She wanted to look away but couldn't make her head turn. Then she saw herself shoot the other Salmmy over and over, there was something wrong about it though. She couldn't put her finger on it. Suddenly she fell forward into the pool, she splashed to the surface to find herself floating in an endless sea.

The sky above was a twisting breathing mass of tiny spots of fire and swirling blues. The spots began to swirl and expand. Small delicate fingers of fire knit them together into a long single line blazing orange. It separated into a multitude of lines, fire in all hues. Insects that have and never will exist crawled up into the sky. They disrupted the smooth movement of the lines causing them to sway and shake. Six thin lines of colour trailing across the sky began to move together sending waves of music throughout the world.

Monks all around began to mirror the song. Molly wondered where they had come from. She looked around and realized she was still sitting in the circle holding her cup of tea.

Mercifully Molly fell asleep before the world became any weirder.

When she awoke the next day she had to hurry for the station or wait another week for the next train. Janet and her daughter Emily were standing on the platform.

'You aren't coming?' Molly asked.

'I think we'll stay for a while.'

Molly started to sign a dozen different things at once, effectively at a loss for words.

'I'll see you next year Molly.' Janet smiled.

The train whistled and the doors began to close. Molly leapt into the train just in time and sat beside the window. She was sure she saw a small streak left behind by her hand as she waved goodbye.

Epilogue...

Salmmy was shouting at the coffee machine when Molly came into the office. He wasn't actually in the office; he was shouting from his room behind his office.
"You defy me at your own peril!!"
The coffee machine did not answer.
"When I get up I am going to melt you down into cups, then I am going to give those cups to someone who likes tea!!"
Molly started making coffee.
"HA!! For the rest of time you shall endure the horrible watery taste of tea!!"
The coffee machine didn't seem overly concerned.
"You're awfully quiet out there... Moll? Are you back?"
Molly walked into his office with a cup of coffee.
"I figured that's why it stopped yelling back." Salmmy sipped his coffee.
Molly glared at him.
"Thanks Moll." He took another sip.
'The ceremony went well.' She signed, still glaring at him.
"I figured as much when I didn't wake up in a film noir situation."
She realised, after a fair bit of trying, that glaring wasn't working. Something about the night at the warehouse kept bothering her and he had promised to explain everything if he lived. So she asked him directly.
'Sammy, why wasn't there any blood on your stomach under the warehouse, I shot you twice.'
"Blanks Moll." He replied nonchalantly.
'What!? When? Then that means...'
"Yeah, he'll be fine."
'Why would you let him live?'
"I owed him my life Moll, it was the least I could do."
'He tried to kill you!'
"No he didn't Moll, he pointed an empty gun at me."
'He didn't know that!'
"Hmm, Yes I suppose that does change things a bit."

'A bit! You're an idiot!'

"Well it all worked out anyway. And technically, He just wanted to take my life, killing me was a means to an end."

'What the hell does that mean?'

"Once I was dead he was going to pretend to be me, I can't blame him."

'Why the hell not!?' Molly was getting really agitated.

"He saved my life, he was just trying to even things up."

'How did he save your life!?'

"A little over four years ago I walked into a trap at that warehouse, I was being cocky and stupid. A bunch of rats were going to kill me when my tail just dropped off and started bouncing around. While they were distracted I ran away and left it behind."

'But you have a tail.'

"Yeah, it grew back."

'Tails do that!?'

"Apparently, anyway I guess from the tails point of view it lost its Sammy."

'You expect me to believe that your tail grew a new Sammy?'

"I'd get him to back me up on it but you did shoot him quite a few times."

'With blanks!' Molly signed angrily.

Salmmy wasn't paying attention though, he was staring out the window watching the last rays of sunset.

They both stared into the darkness for a long time. As the room grew truly dark Molly signed slowly, almost hoping he couldn't see.

'I'm sorry, for everything.'

Salmmy reached over and wiped a tear from her cheek and nodded toward the dark sky that had held an almost perfect sunset, almost.

"Me too."

No Salamanders were harmed in the writing of this book. Except that one time when Salmmy burned his tongue, but that was his own fault.

"No it wasn't"

"Sammy, you tried to drink coffee straight from the pot, what did you think would happen?"

"I thought it would be extra fresh obviously."

"Listen we're done with the book now so you can stop typing. Molly? Molly!"

"Don't bother, she's isn't actually listening, just typing like a reporter reads a teleprompter, blindly." Salmmy smiled like a jackass.

"If she isn't paying attention how did she know you were smiling?"

"Good guess?"

"Fair enough, well I am going to see what's on TV."

-----indistinct voices from the television-----

"Molly! Seriously, quit typing!"

Acknowledgments

I'd like to thank Tom and Toots for listening to my endless rambling about lizards, ow damnit FINE! Salamanders... anyway that and reading the endless revisions that occurred throughout the process.

As a personal note: TOM, FINISH WRITING YOUR DAMN BOOK!

Seriously, he was pitching the idea at the beginning of 2015 and will probably end up publishing around November 2077 at the rate he is going.

and thanks to Baked N' Fresh in Kathmandu for all the coffee and Wi-Fi.

Vagabond Tim
WWW.BINDLESTIFF.CA

Filthy newspaper thief

The moon swam naked, a celestial exhibitionist alone in the inky black sky. Far above the street, not quite so high as the moon but still fairly high up, Salmmy stood before the window in his small apartment attached to his small shabby office. He gazed out onto the street for a long time before turning around slowly to address the prattling old bird.

"So let me make sure I have this right. You want to hire me to find out who is stealing your newspaper."

"Yes, I say yes, this ain't a matter of money son, this here is about principles. I want this little varmints head on a stick in my front yard as a warning!"

"Alright calm down, and just to reiterate, you think that most likely one of the neighborhood kids is stealing your newspaper, and you want me to decapitate him and display his head as a warning to others... I'm not sure you can do that... It seems like the type of thing that's probably illegal."

"Fine. I guess we don't have to kill'em. Can you just rough 'im up a bit?"

"Again, I am pretty sure that even beating a small child is going to cause us some legal problems down the road... Tell you what, I'll find out where your newspaper is disappearing too and let you sort it out from there."

"Can't even throttle the neighbor kid in the street anymore, what is this country coming to." The old warbler complained to no one in particular.

"You are aware that my daily rate is more than a subscription to the newspaper for a year?" Salmmy asked.

"Damnit I don't care what it costs. I told you this is a matter of honour!" The warbler leapt to his feet and started shrieking about vengeance.

"Fine!" Salmmy shouted back. "I'll take your stupid case just to get you out of my office on one condition."

"What condition?" The warbler asked suddenly much calmer.

"I will never speak with you again, ever! When I find out who is taking your paper, you will pay my secretary, and under no circumstances will you come back into my office."

"Fine, what's this gonna cost me?" The warbler asked dejected.

"Fifty a day plus expenses, more if you don't leave right now." Salmmy responded.

Salmmy settled into the chair at his desk and lowered his head The easy solution was to simply buy the stupid bird a new subscription and keep the change. Salmmy reasoned that this wouldn't work as there was always the chance whoever actually was stealing the paper might stop. If the old bird started getting two papers every morning, there was a good chance he would notice. Alternatively, the thief might start stealing the second paper as well in some sort of twisted plot to prevent the warbler from discovering whatever was in the paper. Now that he thought about it he wondered what could be in the paper that the thief didn't want the warbler to see... Satisfied that he had at least one good lead Salmmy pressed the button on the intercom on his desk.

"Hey Molly, can you bring me a copy of the newspaper?" The intercom hissed in annoyance for a moment before Salmmy remembered spilling coffee on it earlier this morning. After deciding that it was still pouting he got up and wandered into the lobby.

Molly, his secretary, was apparently on some sort of mission to open every cupboard and drawer in the office. Salmmy began assisting her by opening the remaining few cupboards before moving to the filing cabinet.

Molly grabbed his shoulder and handed him a quickly scrawled note.

'Where is the coffee pot?'

"Oh, I put it away this morning" he replied cheerfully. Gesturing toward the table next to the coffee machine she handed him another slip of paper.

'No, you didn't. It belongs with the coffee machine'

"You can't keep them in the same place!" Salmmy answered appalled.
Molly's eye twitched a little as she wrote.

    'Why not?'

"Well obviously they can't conspire against me if they are in separate place." Salmmy answered with barely contained condescension.
Before she could respond Salmmy continued "Hey Molly, can you bring me a copy of the newspaper?"
She wrote dejectedly.

    'Which newspaper Salmmy?'

"I need a copy of every newspaper that runs a daily, it is going to be a long afternoon."

Almost an hour later Molly walked into his office with a large stack of papers. Salmmy looked up at her in confusion. He had entirely forgotten that she had left, or that he had asked her to get the papers in the first place. She set the stack on his desk. "Oh never mind those, turns out it was a bad idea, we have work to do, get your coat." Salmmy said from his chair. Molly stormed out of his office, slamming the door behind her. There was a thumping sound from the front office that Salmmy reasoned was more than likely Molly banging her head on her desk, she seemed to have a habit of doing that whenever he asked her to do something that seemed perfectly reasonable. He wondered if she needed some sort of medication.
A few moments later he saw her silhouette in the fogged glass of his office door. She was reaching out and making some sort of strangling motion with her hands. Something was seriously not right with that girl.
When she seemed to be finished choking invisible people in the lobby Salmmy stood up and opened his office door and followed her downstairs to the garage.

Salmmy pulled to a stop down the street from the old warbler's house. He slowly backed the car into an empty driveway where it was hidden by a hedge and still allowed him to see the porch of the house. His view would have been complete except for a large dark van parked in front. The van created a fairly irritating blind spot. While he was debating moving the car Molly interrupted him by handing him a note.

'Why am I here Salmmy?'

"Would you prefer to be at the office in case the phone rings?" he asked sarcastically.
Molly just glared at him.
"Plus, stakeouts are boring and I wanted someone to talk to."
Molly wasn't sure if she should be angry that she had to spend the next few hours looking at an empty porch or that she had to spend the next few hours listening to Salmmy ramble. He read her momentary confusion as an agreement and leaned back in his chair.
"So, the warbler is absolutely mad. He was in my office rambling about murdering some neighborhood kid for stealing his newspaper."

'That's horrible'

"I know right!?"

'Are we waiting for him to leave so we can search his house?'

"Why?"

'For evidence about the child he murdered!'

"What child? He wanted me to kill him, once I found out which one of course."

'Which one what?'

118

Molly was becoming fairly agitated for reasons Salmmy couldn't understand.
"To kill obviously."

>*'How is that obvious! What the (there was a series of angrily scrawled profanity) are you talking about!!?'*

Quite confused as to where she had stopped following the conversation Salmmy decided it was best to simply change the subject.
"Never mind, the point is we are here to find out who is stealing his newspaper." Salmmy stated flatly.
Molly took several slow deep breaths before writing again.

>*'Salmmy, why do we care who is stealing his newspaper?'*

"That's the point of the whole case!" Salmmy replied testily.
Molly reached into her pocket to retrieve a small card. She had started making them in large numbers a month ago using a stamp she had purchased. She often found she was repeating herself. She handed the card to Salmmy.
'I need more of those cards' she thought.
Salmmy looked down at the now familiar card, it contained only three little words.

>*I HATE YOU.*

Salmmy shook his head and stared off towards the van. The driver was seated inside reading a newspaper. Salmmy approached the door calmly and rapped on the window. it rolled down slowly, stopping halfway.
"What do you want?" the mouse asked without looking up from his paper.
"How long have you been watching the house down the road, and have you been stealing this guy's newspaper the entire time?" Salmmy asked gesturing towards his client's house with his thumb.
"Who says I am watching a house?"
"Salmmy does, well I do, hmm that's confusing let me start

over. I'm Salmmy and I said you are." He answered politely. There was a long pause while the man in the van slowly shifted from confusion to annoyance.

"Idiot" he replied while slowly raising the window.

"It rained early this morning, the spot under your van is dry, you have been reading the same page for the entire half-hour that I've been watching you, from where you are sitting you have a clear view of the front door and the side of the house while not being overly conspicuous. Look I could go on but you are about to be covered in shattered glass" Salmmy watched as the window continued upwards, he tapped the butt of his gun against the window and smiled again. Taking his meaning the window rolled down.

"I'm a private dick, I am working here, so piss off before you call more attention to me!" the man shifted in his seat as he spoke.

"The bird whose paper you are reading is a crazy person, he is paying me to find out who is stealing it." Salmmy replied matter of factly.

"So if I stop stealing the paper you will go away?" The mouse asked hopefully.

"Oh no, not at all. He is paying me daily for as long as it takes to find out who is stealing it, keep stealing it for as long as you need, just call me when your case is solved so I can tell my client."

"That doesn't strike you as unethical?"

"You're the one watching an empty house for a client who asked you to keep an eye on his wife, how is that any better?"

"What the hell are you talking about, she hasn't left in days, and who says I am watching anyone."

"Still me, still Salmmy. By the way I never did catch your name." Salmmy said.

"I, wait, what!?" The man in the van was clearly beginning to get quite agitated.

"Look, I know you're a detective so I don't want to tell you how to do your job. Well I guess you did just tell me how to do mine, but I'll take the high road here. I am sure you noticed that there are three soggy newspapers in front of the house. I am equally sure you know this house belongs to Captain

Jimmy, and that he is currently in the middle of a pretty ugly territorial dispute with another smuggler. What I can't figure out is why, given this information, you are watching an empty house."

The man in the van grew very pale. Finally, he began to speak. "I didn't know, I swear it." He began to blubber and ceased making sense.

"You misunderstand, I'm not here to kill you. If Jimmy knew you were here I am sure he would have sent someone... Honestly I thought you were quite brave, until I realized you're just stupid."

The engine roared to life and the van sped away. Salmmy shrugged and walked back to his car.

"Well that was a waste of time." He complained.

'What happened? Who was in the van?'

"Some newspaper thief posing as a detective. The real pain of it is that now I need to drive down here every morning to steal the newspaper myself or I stop getting paid."

Plans for tomorrow

I'm going to kill him.
Supposedly he gets killed all the time and 'gets better' but I have no evidence of this. Just to be sure though I am going to kill him extra hard, in the face.

As usual I started work by unlocking the door at nine, we never have any clients but it's a matter of principle. An hour later Salmmy staggered out of his office.
"What time is it?"
'Ten.'
"What day is it?"
'Tuesday.'
"Why isn't there coffee, don't we open at nine?"
I was going to throw something at him but the phone rang. I hate that thing.
I can't talk so basically I just listen to someone become increasingly desperate for a response until they hang up, then I tell Salmmy who I think it probably was, it's not a good system.
This time it was Franklin on the phone, he knows the routine so he just waited quietly while I buzzed his name into the intercom.
..−. .−. .−ˉ −. ˉ.− .−.. .. ˉ.
I transferred Franklin and headed over to make coffee. We have an absolutely absurd and wildly impractical bezzera that Salmmy refuses to learn how to use. Since he drinks his

bodyweight in coffee every day I make a LOT of coffee and have grown to hate it fiercely.

I hate it because that giant gold tube is almost as tall as I am and sits on a really low table so all the cups and stuff I need is just out of reach. That and the fact that I'm not a damn waitress. I didn't go to university for this! I studied archeology. I studied art history. Now that I see that in writing I realize I am sort of lucky to have a job at all.

I blew a bunch of steam on the handle of the cup after putting it on the tray to make sure it was ridiculously hot and headed into his office. The window on his office door is frosted so I couldn't actually see Salmmy coming until the door flew open and threw the tray and coffee all over me.

"No time for coffee Moll, we have to go to the morgue."

That's another thing, he refuses to say my name. It's MOLLY you jackass.

'Why?' I sign.

"I swear this time there is actually a dead body." He assures me.

'So what! You just want to waste a day hanging out with your weird friend Mike, why should I come?'

"This one was murdered."

'Fine, let me go change.'

"No time, you look fine."

'I'm dripping coffee!'

"Good point, here take my jacket so you don't get any on the seats." He threw his coat at me and bounded off down the stairs. It's kind of odd but I have noticed recently that he moves differently when there are other people around. It's like a kind of forced nonchalance. When it's just us he makes no effort to hide the fact that he is an idiot kid posing as an adult. Not wanting to walk down six flights of stairs I walked up the wall to my apartment and changed while I waited for the elevator. A few minutes later I got to the basement to find Salmmy sitting in the car revving the engine.

The first few times I saw him do this I thought he was being impatient, that was until I opened the car door before he saw me and heard him making car noises as he cranked the wheel around. Now I realize he is just... lets go with eccentric.

As soon as I sat down, before I had a chance to even close the door, he roared off into the street. It's a great car I have to admit. He stole it from this weasel about a year ago when he somehow, and I am quoting here, killed his old car with a bookshelf. I have no idea what that means but trust me when I tell you that getting him to explain something is almost never worth the effort.

We pulled to a stop in front of a fairly disreputable looking ice cream parlour. I didn't think there WERE disreputable ice cream parlours until I saw this place. The metal shutters were locked closed with several different rust covered locks, the shutters themselves were covered in graffiti, and the most disturbing sign was actually the sign that claimed they sold "Ice cream." Those quotes made me fairly nervous.

"What flavour?"

'I don't want ice cream, I thought we had to go to the morgue.'

"We do, but I need to see someone first and it will look pretty suspicious if I don't get ice cream. So what flavour?"

'Strawberry I guess.'

The fact that this was easily the sketchiest possible place to get ice cream didn't seem to bother him, neither did the complete absence of other customers. Which of course rendered his argument about looking suspicious completely pointless but he had already left before I had a chance to point it out. A few minutes later he saunters out of the door carrying two cones of chocolate ice cream.

'Pretty sure I said strawberry.'

"You did, and it was a great guess, but it turns out you were wrong." Then he hands me a cone. Since I use my hands for talking and there is nowhere to set the damn thing there is nothing I can say.

Almost instantly he inhaled his entire cone and spent the next two minutes pounding his fist on the dash and shouting every piece of profanity he has ever encountered. Finally, when the ice cream headache passed he started driving to what I assumed would be the morgue. I was wrong. Somehow he managed he accelerate every time I tried to take a bite of ice cream so I ended up with frozen chocolate impacted into my snout.

When we stopped he looked over and laughed as though it wasn't completely his fault and then hopped out of the car. I was in no hurry to catch up so I took a moment to clear my nostrils and fix my face. When I did step out of the car I realized we were not actually at the morgue. We were at an optometrist's office for some reason.

Neither of us wears glasses so I assumed he was asking about the case. Just as I was about to go in and see what was taking him so long he bounded out of the door and started whining about delays and how I should have been waiting in the car. I thought about shooting him right there in the parking lot but he was already in the car being impatient.

Finally, mercifully we got to the morgue. He stopped the car and actually waited for me, which made me suspicious.

-Tim's Note-
Molly tends to get a little caught up in typing and will write down anything she hears. It's weird and makes this next bit a little confusing.

"NOOO!!! You'll ruin it, Tim make her stop, she'll ruin it." Salmmy whined upwards.
"Ruin what, Molly what are you doing?" Tim replied from the couch where he couldn't possibly see my hands.
"She's telling them the morgue thing!"
"Ok, so what's the problem?"
"You've listened to her stories, they're terrible."
"I think you got to say enough in the book."
"Tell her to make coffee and I'll finish it."
"You can't type though; you mean you'll keep complaining until I finish it don't you."
Salmmy began poking Molly in the shoulder with the tip of his tail.
"Same thing, hey you, make coffee."
Molly stormed off snoofily.
"Hey I think she got ahead of herself, she wrote that she stormed off... and the stuff I'm saying right now... I'm scared.

-Tim's note
As somewhat explained in the above bit of strangeness I will
be finishing the story due to Salmmy being a whiny jerk.

Salmmy held the door for her as she went in, she eyed him
suspiciously the entire time. The bodies are kept three stories
down in a refrigerated room that seemed to lack vents. The
smell was in a word unpleasant.
"Hey Mike." Salmmy chirped happily, he was always slightly
too enthusiastic about this part of the job.
"What?" The shabby mouse, known to his friends as Mike
despite the nametag that read Charles, seemed to have been
sleeping.
"We're here for the body."
"That gang thing?"
This didn't seem right to Molly; she couldn't say exactly why
but this had all the hallmarks of one of Salmmy's ridiculously
complicated lies that seemed funny only to him.
"Yes, also shut up."
"Uhuh…" Mike opened the drawer and slid out the
exceptionally flat body of a guinea pig.
"So Moll, what do you see?"
She absolutely hated this game, it was just an excuse for
Salmmy to gloat over some trivial detail she had overlooked.
'It's Molly.' She signed before looking closely at the body.
'Well, two sets of tire tracks, not the front and back tires
though.'
Molly looked at Salmmy waiting for a response. He just
nodded back towards the body.
'The tracks are from the same car though, whoever drove over
him circled around to hit him again?'
When she looked up she saw that Salmmy had produced from
somewhere a set of dark sunglasses that he proceeded to take
off dramatically as he spoke.
"So you might say he was, re-tired." His smile was short lived
when no one made any indication that they had found this
funny. Molly threw his coat off her shoulders and hurled it at
him before storming off.

"C'mon, that was funny." Salmmy pleaded with Mike. "I've been holding onto that since Franklin told me about this guy this morning."

"Aren't you worried she'll leave without you?"

Salmmy reached into his coat pocket intent on smugly displaying the car keys. His pocket though, turned out to be empty.

He reached the parking lot just in time to see his car, and his secretary, roaring off into the street.

Hiking with Lars

I first met lars in a Tibetan restaurant surrounded by trees full of chattering squirrels. He was covered in paint, as is his custom.

Since I don't speak squirrel as well as I would like I didn't follow their argument as well as I would have liked. He explained that I had wandered into a lively political debate regarding the equal distribution of trees resulting in the unequal distribution of nuts. I informed him that they were clearly all nuts and went back to eating my lunch.

For those of you who don't know him I should mention that Lars is a squirrel. A smallish grey squirrel, well grey wherever there is not paint. Mostly he is a squirrel shaped object covered in flecks of paint spewing a surprising amount of nonsense with the diction of a college professor. Also he wears a headband.

So this little squirrel hopped down from a tree and landed on my table with a thud and a small shower of paint chips that landed on the food I was attempting to eat.

"You shouldn't eat that!" He said.

"Because of the paint?" I asked

"Because it had a face!" He exclaimed excitedly.

"My sandwich did not have a face." I explained as I tried to get the waiter's attention.

"The meat in it did!" I began to wonder if he was capable of speaking without exclamation marks.

"So I should only eat vegetables then?" I asked.

"Well, not really, if you did that what would the things with faces eat..."

"So what should I eat then?" I asked

"I actually don't know; it is one of the topics on today's agenda." He managed without exclaiming.

"Alright then, I'll get another sandwich, without paint on it, and when you figure it out you can come back down and let me know."

He seemed to accept this idea and happily scampered back up

the tree beside my table.

The chittering noises continued to grow louder for about an hour as I sat with my now empty new plate and a cup of coffee and watched them. Occasionally a squirrel would hop from one tree to another, I assume because he found their arguments persuasive, or perhaps they just like leaping.
After I had finished my coffee I became a bit bored and stood up to go. I was startled by a sudden weight on my shoulders, also the claws the sudden weight used to make sure it stayed on my shoulder. Until that moment I had never considered that squirrels had vicious little claws, but now I knew.
I turned my head and looked at Lars who was excitedly dancing on my shoulder amid a few slowly growing spots of blood.
"We decided!" He exclaimed.
"That's great Lars, so what should I eat?"
"I'll show you, it isn't far."
"You can't just tell me?"
"No, it's easier this way, c'mon."
I should have realized then that when he said easier he meant for him, easier because he was riding on a shoulder while I was trudging through mountainous terrain.
I should also note that writers are not generally well known for physical fitness, in fact most of us can get winded answering the phone.

Four hours and half a million hills later he began to assure me that it was
"Just over this hill."
Or
"Just a few more minutes."
By this point I was hopelessly lost and had no choice but to continue following his squirrely directions.
"You know Lars; I could eat a squirrel if I had too." I muttered bitterly.
"Who?"
"What?"
"Which squirrel?" He asked.

"Any squirrel I suppose, if I was hungry enough." I answered.
"Oh good, I was worried I might know him."
"If this hike takes much longer you might find that you know him very well." I said smiling evilly at him.
"I thought you were lost though." He said.
"I am!"
"How do you expect to meet a squirrel I know very well when you don't even know where you are?"
"Never mind Lars, how much further?"
"Just over this hill!" He lied cheerfully.
Several hours later we found ourselves at the very same restaurant that we had been at this morning.
"Damnit Lars, why did we walk around all day just to end up back here!?"
"Well... You were going to leave and we hadn't gotten to the food thing yet."
"Then what was all that arguing while I was eating."
"We were deciding how to stall you while we figured it out." He replied.
Struggling against the urge to smash him into small painty squirrel bits I asked as calmly as I could
"So did they decide while we were gone?"
Lars shuffled his feet and looked down before muttering
"No."
"Why not!"
"Well you see, I am the committee chair today so when I left, the meeting ended."
"Then why did you come with me to stall me instead of sending someone else?"
"We voted."
"You voted to stop the meeting while you stalled me until the meeting was over!?"
"I voted no! Frankly you're terrible company, I wanted to spend the day making protest signs." He replied indignantly.

Tim refuses to understand that morse code makes no sense to most people so I added the little sheet here after he was done editing the book. Just be cool and don't tell him ok.
-Molly

A	.-
B	-...
C	-.-.
D	-..
E	.
F	..-.
G	--.
H	....
I	..
J	.---
K	-.-
L	.-..
M	--
N	-.
O	---
P	.--.
Q	--.-
R	.-.
S	...
T	-
U	..-
V	...-
W	.--
X	-..-
Y	-.--
Z	--..

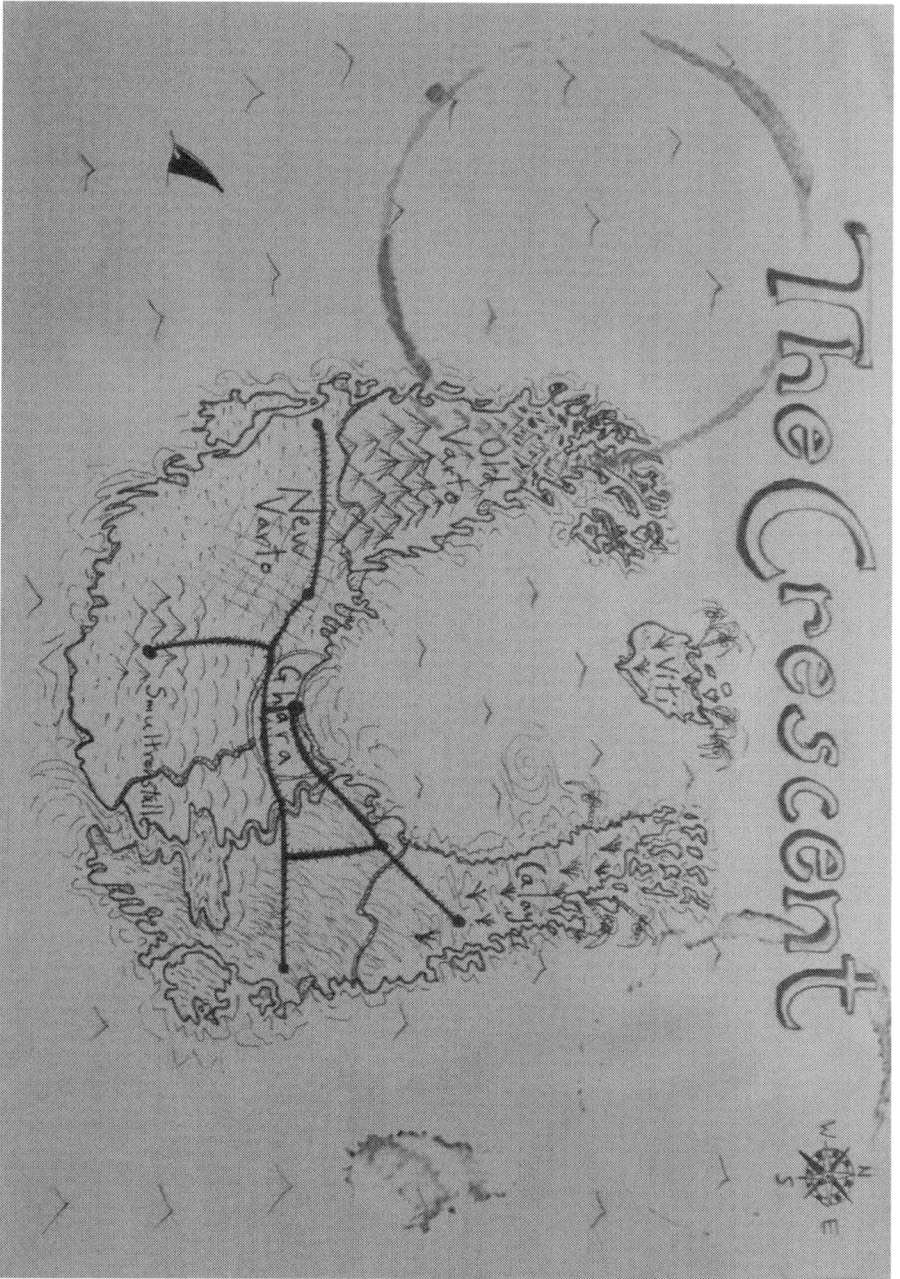

The Crescent

Manufactured by Amazon.ca
Bolton, ON